The Alphabet Books: ABC

Marc Richard

Copyright © 2017 Marc Richard

All rights reserved.

ISBN:1545567115
ISBN-13:9781545567111

DEDICATION

For my Crew: Marla Alvather, Gayle Armstrong, David Berg, Curtis Bushart, Marshall Clowers, Ari Cohen, Steve Cohen, Chris Coleman, Kelly Connerton, Rhonda Corson, Alex Cunningham, Johannes Debler, Tony Dodds, Tere Fredericks, Tam French, Emily G., Teddy Garrett, Anne Marie Kaczorowksi, Pam Lea, Larry Marek, Mike Meredith, Norma Miles, Bob Newman, Quentin Norman, Crystal Organ, Caleb Orion, Elizabeth Peacock, Nick Perry, Martha Reed, Steve Roberts, Kym Russell, Michael Shulman, Michelle Sime, Dawn Taylor, Virna Thibault, Jill Thibodeau, Justin Tyler, Charly Urban, Craig Ware, Ron Wells, Papa Woodie, Art, Bri, Lori, Megan, Melissa, Pati, Raymond, Rich, and Roberta. Thank you for making this possible.

A IS FOR ADAM

1	The Sixth Day	6
2	The Belladonna Chronicles	10
3	Eve	14
4	Tiptoe Through the Garden	20
5	Another Day for You and Me in Paradise	24
6	That's a Lot of Trouble for a Pie	31
7	Confession	38
8	Eden's End	44
9	Gifts From Heaven	49
10	Seeds	57
11	Sometimes You Gotta Make Do	62
12	Belly	67
13	What Is Wrong with These Kids Today?	73
14	Tigris	79
15	Meanwhile, on the Left Bank…	83
16	Eve's Restless Night	90
17	A Talk with the Boys	96
18	Trees	100

B IS FOR BEAR

1	That's Amore!	1
2	Meet the DiFrenzos	6
3	The Twat-Waffle Diaries	11
4	Blondie	17
5	Who's the Bimbo?	25
6	Porridge	34
7	It's Good for Stains, Though	42
8	Your Ma Made Lasagna	49
9	The Blue Iguana	53
10	Meatballs	61
11	Gabagool	66
12	St. Mark's	71
13	Awfully Sorry	76
14	I Don't Know but I Don't Feel So Good	84
15	I Don't Know What You Mean, I Feel Great!	87
16	The Back Room	93
17	Don Figarazzi	101
18	The Docks	103

C IS FOR COOKIE

1	That's Good Enough for Me	6
2	Celebrate Good Times	12
3	Tom Waits	16
4	Just Cookies	27
5	The Truth About Dad	33
6	The Irving Station	40
7	cookies	53
8	COOKIES!	58
9	Birds and Breadcrumbs	64
10	Ranger Rick	73
11	The Chocolate River	80
12	Delivery	86
13	Magic	95
14	Epilogue	102

A is for Adam

1. The Sixth Day

A bug crawled across his face, waking him up.

"All right, all right. I'm up. Jesus." He wasn't sure who Jesus was, since he was the only living human in the Universe; it just seemed like the right thing to say. The bug crawled across his face every morning around this time, so he never overslept. He wasn't sure what would happen if he did oversleep, since he didn't have a job. He rolled over to check the alarm clock by his nightstand. But there was no alarm clock. Or nightstand. Or time.

The bug was hungry. Adam found a large bright green leaf, picked it up off the ground, blew off the dirt that had accumulated on it, and set it in front of his bug friend. Why the insect couldn't find his own damned food was beyond him. But his was not to question the ways of the Universe.

He needed to get dressed and start his day. The garden needed watering, and it wasn't like anyone else was going to do it. He opened the top drawer of his bureau, which was full of several different versions of the same piece of clothing: A leaf, like the one he just fed the bug, with a vine tied in a large loop through it. There was really no need for clothing, since modesty was a thing of the future. No, this wasn't out of modesty at all. This was totally utilitarian, to keep the sheep from nobbling at his privates. He had made several hundred versions of these leaf clothes , mostly out of boredom, and on the last few, he figured out how to make the knot adjustable in case he gained or lost weight. There were plenty of animals for him to slaughter, so he never had to go hungry, but it was a giant pain to have to constantly kill the animals, prepare them, and cook them, every single day. So some days he went without eating and lost a little weight. Fruits and vegetables were abundant, but they did very little to keep the weight on. Plus, he was getting pretty sick of the lack of variety.

One food he was curious about was the Fruit that hung from the special tree in the center of the garden. He was very tempted to eat one, just to see what it tasted like, since it looked delicious. But God said no. He was never sure why God said no. Something about how the tree possessed knowledge, and if he ate the fruits that blossomed from it, he would suddenly know things. At first it all sounded a little like science fiction to him, and a lot like bullshit. And so what if he did know things? What was the harm in that? But who was he to question God? Soon, however, he began to believe that maybe there was some truth to this knowledge thing after all. He often caught one of the goats eating a fallen Fruit from the Tree, and he was beginning to believe that the goat was becoming smarter than him. It had even learned how to walk on its hind legs, and was beginning to speak Arabic. This seemed a little too close to evolution, and he was quite surprised that God didn't put a stop to that right away. If this kept up, soon the monkeys may start turning into people. And that was some real messed up stuff. He stared at the Tree. Some day he was going to eat one of those Fruits. He'd be damned if he was going to be outwitted by a goat.

He stood at the edge of his garden, watering it. And a very large garden it was. Although large compared to what, he wasn't quite sure. There were fig trees and pear trees, juniper bushes and blueberry bushes. He would have been quite proud of it, were pride not a sin. It was beautiful, if he did say so himself, and he took great pains to make it that way. If any visitors did show up, they would be greeted with the most amazing sights and intoxicating smells. He had enough to feed an army, and it was a shame to let this all be for nothing. He couldn't help but feel that it was all quite wasteful. No matter; it wasn't he that was wasting it. It was whomever created this garden. Was that a sin to think that? He hoped not. So far, he was without sin, and he wished to keep it that way.

He had never been far enough out into the garden to lose sight of his own hut, so he had no idea just how massive it was. He had plenty to eat all around him, and there was no need to venture out any farther. But he was sure there was more to see way out there. More delights and wonderments that he hadn't discovered yet. So why not? He was curious, as well as bored. He was hoping curiosity and boredom weren't sins; he couldn't wait until God came out with a list or handbook or something.

2. The Belladonna Chronicles

He left behind the figs and junipers and little prepackaged bags of cashews. Farther and farther in he went, till soon he lost sight of his hut. He hoped he didn't get lost, but then again, home was where you hung your fig leaf, so he could set up shop anywhere he liked, really.

Such sights were there to greet him! Strange green objects and yellow ones and brown ones. Things he had never seen before, not even in his craziest dreams. Why hadn't he ventured out before today? He could have been eating all these delicious-looking things. He strolled around, naming things as he went, because that was the privilege he had by being the only human in existence. He called this one kiwi and that one coconut, this one clam and that one olive, this one cucumber and that one Doug. On and on he strolled through the garden, tasting a little of this, a little of that. Some things were perfect right off the vine, like the things he now called grapes. Other things obviously needed to be cooked, such as the large, orange object he decided for some cute reason to call pumpkin. Of course, due to his naivety, it never occurred to him that some things were not edible, and were just there to be admired only with the eyes, such as nice, innocent-looking fruit that resembled what he called blueberries. He decided to name these belladonna, after the lead singer of Anthrax. Hmm. They tasted pretty decent. A little sweet. He picked them, one by one, off the vine, shoving them into his mouth as he did so.

It briefly entered his mind that maybe he should save room for other treats, he was sure there would be more farther on, but the more he ate of these, the better they tasted. He felt like a glutton. He wasn't sure what a glutton was, but he pictured one in his mind. It resembled a beaver, with larger teeth and a pisspoor attitude. It scampered around and around the belladonna, a shrub, looking to take a bite out of Adam's bare foot. He kicked the creature, which sprouted wings midair and flew away to better things. The berries jumped off the bush and shot into his mouth and started burning with the heat of a thousand suns. The ground opened up beneath him and threatened to swallow him whole. Cthulu's tentacles shot up out of the earth and wrapped themselves around him. He felt comforted by the sweet caresses, as he was lifted higher and higher into the stratosphere. Who in the world is Cthulu? He thought, and when he realized he had no idea, this caused the tentacles that held him fast to go bye bye, dropping him from thousands of feet in the air. The ground was approaching fast, and he briefly got a glimpse of his future face looking like a plate of corned beef hash. Suddenly, he remembered the parachute he had on his back that he had earlier fashioned out of pterodactyl skin, and he pulled the rip cord. It occurred to him at that moment that he had inadvertently packed the beak in the deployment bag instead of the skin. Faster and faster he plummeted to the earth, and as he was approaching his inevitable demise, structures began rising up out of the ground, shooting straight skyward. His beak-achute caught on the antenna at the top of one of the structures, but not before the cord wrapped itself around his neck, and he hung there, thousands of feet in the air, strangling. A giant monkey, seeing his dilemma, began climbing the structure. He made it quickly to the top, and began punching airplanes out of the sky. Never mind the airplanes, save me! He thought but could not say, as he was choking to death. The monkey crabbed the cord, untangled it from the antenna, and climbed back down the structure, setting him gently on the ground. He turned and stomped away. Wait, monkey! How can I repay you? But with just a few strides, the monkey was already in the next zip code. A massive explosion rocked the ground, and the structures all came crashing down. The apocalypse happened much sooner than he had expected. Oh well, he thought, at least I have all these books to read. But he stumbled, and his glasses fell off his face. But wait! He didn't wear glasses. What the hell were glasses? Glass had not been invented yet, but he did have a pair of spectacles that he fashioned out of plastic cups. He had 15/20 vision, but no other people in existence also meant no scales, vision or otherwise. All he knew was that when he put those plastic cups up to his eyes, he saw better. Especially when he put a little water in them, as a refractor.

That's the last thought he had before he collapsed in the garden, fast asleep.

3. Eve

He awoke hours later, wrapped warmly in a kangaroo pelt blanket, and a recently deceased bunny under his head as a pillow. He should have been comfortable, for this was his preferred way of sleeping; however, he was not. Something was not quite right. For one, he was way out in the middle of the garden, probably lost. Who covered him up? This also didn't feel like his usual bunny, since he'd had his bunny pillow for a long time, and it was broken in exactly the way he liked it. This bunny seemed too new. Too stiff, which made his head cock at a strange angle, giving him a crick in his neck.

Another thing that was bothering him was this annoying pain in his side. He reached down and touched where the sensation was coming from. This didn't feel right at all. Flinging the blanket aside, he got a good look at his body. What the heck? A huge gash in his side was dripping blood onto the dirt. Kidney thieves! He thought, and plunged his hand inside the opening. Everything seemed fine, pretty much. His heart was still there. His lungs were still there, although he could have figured that out without feeling them, since he was breathing. He reached all the way around, straining his elbow as he did so, and felt for his kidneys. One, two. Both there. Well, that sure was a relief. Although he knew he could have lived with just one kidney, he preferred to have both of them, in case something came up. Pulling his arm back, his hand noticed something on the way out. Or rather, the lack of something. He was missing a rib. There it was, the portion where it was broken off, sticking out like a snapped tree limb.

"Hey, would you mind giving me back the covers?" came a sweet-sounding voice. "I'm freezing over here."

Someone was lying right next to him. How did he not notice that before? Probably the whole gash thing was making it hard to be aware of anything else . This was the first person he'd ever met, besides himself.

"Steve?" Adam asked

"Eve," the person answered.

"Haha! Hurrah! Praise Yahweh! Our Creator has finally given me a companion!" He suddenly looked remorseful. "Sorry I haven't had any time to clean the place up. I wasn't expecting company."

"Quite all right," Eve responded. "I mean, the world is a rather large place for one person to keep tidy."

His eyes fell to her chest. "Yes, I suppose it is," he said, distractedly.

"Umm, can I help you?" Eve asked.

"You'll have to excuse my eyes. They have a mind of their own."

"Quite all r..."

"What are those???" he asked, excitedly.

"Those are boobies. They are our Creator's gift to you."

"Do they hurt?"

"No, not really. They just add a little weight to my front side, is all. Does that hurt?" she asked, pointing to his thing he had yet to name. He thought of calling it a glumph, but he wasn't sure. Sometimes, especially when it got really cold, it felt like a plink.

"No, does yours?" he asked, and looked down at his

midsection. "Oh, pardon me. Where is my fig leaf?"

She pointed to her own crotch area. "I borrowed yours. Sorry for not asking, but I thought you were dead. You weren't responding and you were bleeding quite heavily."

"No problem. I have several of them back at the house. And I wasn't dead, I was just completely wasted. Do yourself a favor and stay away from the things that look like blueberries but aren't blueberries."

"I don't even know what blueberries are, so it'll be hard for me to stay away from the things that look like them but aren't them."

"Don't worry, I'll show you around. Now, you still haven't answered my question."

"Which was?" she asked.

"Does your glumph hurt?"

"I don't have one," she answered, turning six shades of red.

"What do you mean, you don't have one?" he asked.

She moved the fig leaf aside a little, so he could see what was down there. He'd seen those before on other animals, and often thought of putting his thing in them, after watching other animals put their things in them, but he was embarrassed that he just didn't measure up. But here was one he may be able to get into, after some persuasion and perhaps a few cups of fermented grape juice.

"I'm sorry, are you disappointed?" she asked.

"Oh no no, not at all," he said, turning a few shades of red himself. "I like the fact that you have one of those. I call them squash blossoms."

"That's kind of cute," she said, and rolled her eyes.

"Say, what do I call you, anyway?" he asked.

"As I have said, you can call me Eve," she said.

"Yes, but what are you, one who is almost like me yet different?"

"I am called woman. Meaning from man. The Creator took your rib and used it to make me."

"What?" he asked.

"Yeah, sounds kind of like witchery to me. But who are we to question? Anyhow, I have come from you, and am not original, therefore I will always be less than you and subservient to you. If I ever begin acting autonomous or start speaking my own mind, you are commanded to strike me down with a switch, but not one any larger than your thumb." She looked down at his crotch again. "Or your glumph."

"Sounds like a sweet deal," he answered.

"It is," she answered. "Enjoy it while you can. In thousands of years, this arrangement will change."

"Yeah, I doubt it."

4. Tiptoe Through the Garden

"So, Riblet, here's the Garden," said Adam. "It's pretty nice, if I do say so myself. Bountiful bounties and plentiful plenties, and all that."

"It's Eve," Eve insisted. "Please don't call me Riblet."

"But it's cute," Adam said. "Just like you."

"Flattery will get you nowhere with me. Just remember, Eve. Not Riblet. I don't call you Dirt."

"Hey, hey, now. I'm very sensitive about that. So, I'm made out of dirt; so what? If anything, you can call me Clay, if you want. That sounds more like a name to me. But please don't call me Dirt. In fact," he said, "Adam would be preferable. What are you doing?"

Eve was carving words in the sand with a stick.

ADAM + EVE 4EVA

"Seriously?" he asked. "Already with the sappy stuff?"

She grabbed him painfully by the upper arm, her nails digging into his flesh. "Listen, you little twerp. I don't like this anymore than you do. There I was, floating around in the Ether, and all of a sudden God decides to yank a rib out of some schmuck and use it to turn me into his companion. Someone to keep him company for all eternity. That's my sole job. I'll never be a doctor or a lawyer or an executive at a big corporation with a nice big office on the top floor with a view. I'll just be a sidekick. I'm lucky I even got a name. Believe me, first opportunity I get to burrow my way out of your life, I'm taking it. Till then, It's ADAM

+ EVE 4EVA. Get it?"

"Wow, I'm sorry. Here." Adam handed her a slice of pumpkin, which she chewed for a brief second, then spat out. "Bleccch. That's horrible. What are you trying to do, poison me?"

"Poison you? My only companion till the end of time? No way. I just kind of wanted a second opinion on this lousy fruit."

"Well, it's terrible."

"Agreed. But look what I did." He pointed over to another pumpkin sitting in the garden, minding its own business. A crude face was carved into it.

"I don't get it," she said.

"What's not to get? It's art."

"What's art?" she asked.

"A concept I invented. It's where you create something out of something else."

"That's blasphemy," said Eve. "Only God can create something out of something else."

"Well, obviously that's not true," he said. "I mean, just look at this face," he pointed to the pumpkin again. "And anyway, God created something out of nothing, like the Universe, but it was something useful. Art is really not useful at all."

"So if it's not useful, why do it?"

"It's meant to make people happy. Or sad. Or just evoke any kind of emotion at all. Maybe, in that way, it is useful."

"Well, I think it's dumb."

"I think it'll catch on," said Adam.

"Catch on with whom?" she asked.

"I don't know. Maybe there will be other people some day. I have ribs to spare, after all. Anyway, I think art is pretty cool. Especially this, um, Jack O'Lantern."

"Jack O'Lantern?"

"Yeah, I think it sounds Irish, don't you?"

"What's Irish?" she asked.

"Never mind."

"Personally, I think it's a waste of food," said Eve.

"So?" he answered. "What else are we going to do with it? Besides, is wasting food really all that bad?"

"I'm not sure," she said. "I guess I don't know the difference between good and bad."

"Yes," he said. "If only there was a way to know the difference between good and bad..."

"Yes," she said. "If only."

"Look, things here aren't so terrible. Plenty of delicious things to eat, pumpkin aside, lots of privacy, I mean, lots of privacy, and just look around you."

She did.

"Breathtaking, huh?"

"I guess I could do worse. It is pretty nice."

"This is all ours. To do with as we please. Look, I know it was probably really cool being formless floating around in the Ether, but you're here now. Let's make the best of it. Come on, what do you say? ADAM + EVE 4...?"

"Eva," she said, somewhat bashfully. Maybe it wouldn't be so bad after all.

5. Another Day for You and Me in Paradise

They entered the warm confines of the hut.

"Come on, who's in the mood for some delicious grub?" Adam asked.

Eve looked off in the distance in silence.

"I said, who's in the mood for some delicious grub?"

Eve's head swiveled. "Oh, were you talking to me just now?"

"Who else would I be talking to?" Asked Adam.

"Precisely," she said. "I'm the only other one here. Therefore, your question is stupid."

"Is this what I have to look forward to?" Adam muttered to himself.

"What was that?" Asked Eve.

"I said, who's in the mood for some delicious grub?"

Eve sighed. "Fine. Me. I am."

"All righty, then. Give me time to prepare. Take some time. Explore the grounds."

"You cook?" she asked.

"Yes, I do. And I'm pretty good, if I do say so myself. Although, soon this will change, as you'll be doing all the cooking. As well as dusting the cobwebs, vacuuming the dirt, and ironing my fig leaves with a hot rock. What do you think about that? Sweet deal, huh?"

"Can I go back to being a rib?" asked Eve.

"What, and deny me the precious gift our Lord has

given to me? No thank you. I'd much rather be short a rib. Besides, you know what they say guys are able to do once they have ribs removed?"

"Enlighten me," Eve said.

"Well, umm... I uh... Well, I have you now, so I guess I don't have to worry about it."

"Ha. We'll see about that."

"Aww, well, I think once you try my cooking, you'll think differently," said Adam.

Eve gave Adam a look for the first time. It wasn't a look he liked at all, but it was one that, in the future, men would learn to fear.

"Uh, anyway, why don't you go for a walk? It's a beautiful day today. Go climb some trees, hit a rock with a stick, eat some fruit."

"Yeah, I think it may do me some good to get some alone time."

"Already?" Adam said. "It hasn't even been a whole day."

"Well, you know. Give it time." And with that, she left the hut.

She made her way back through the garden, sampling this and that. One thing she found out, is there were certain things that she loved and certain things she detested. For instance, the thing that Adam called banana (which, Adam had confessed, he ran out of ideas, and just started throwing letters together) was delicious. The thing that Adam called onion was absolutely terrible.

"Adam?" she shouted, and he poked his head out of the window.

"Yes, dear?"

"That onion is just terrible. Absolutely awful. Who in the world would ever eat such a thing?"

"Ah, yes. True. The onion is wretched," Adam said, then added: "But wait till you try it cooked. It's like a whole different food."

"I'll take your word for it," she muttered.

A few more steps later, and there, in front of her, was the Tree. It certainly didn't look very magical. It looked like any of the others, except for the Fruit hanging from it. Though even the Fruit didn't look particularly extraordinary to her, other than the fact that this was the only tree that had grown them. Based strictly on looks, it was nothing she felt she just had to eat. What was intriguing, however, was the fact that God told Adam not to eat from the Tree. The strange powers this Fruit had, bestowing on the consumer a great knowledge, particularly the ultimate knowledge of Good and Evil, that was something that made it hard to resist. Why was that such a bad thing? And why would God place the Tree there with the sole purpose of not eating from it? Temptation? It didn't make sense. Was God a trickster?

"Did I hear ssssomeone ssssay that they wanted to know of Good and Evil?" hissed a voice from the tree.

"Did I say that?" she asked.

"Yessss, you did," the voice said.

"I don't remember saying that," she said.

"Well, you did."

"Hmph. Show yourself, creature."

A long, green slithery thing made its way out around the branch so she could get a good look at it.

"Adam!" she shouted.

His head poked out of the window again. "I'm trying to make a pie," he shouted back. "What is it now?"

"Why is this garden hose talking to me?" she asked.

"That's not a garden hose. It's a snake."

"Then why is this snake talking to me?"

"I think he's Satan," Adam yelled.

"Oh, well that makes sense. Get thee behind me, Satan," she spoke. And with that, the snake was gone from the tree, and crept up from behind her onto her shoulder.

"Aaah! Don't sneak up on someone like that!" she yelled.

"Ssssorry, but you ssssaid..."

"I know what I said. It's a figure of speech."

"Oh. And anyway, I'm not Ssssatan," he whispered in her ear. "I'm just a sssssnake."

"Nuh-uh. No way. You... you're Evil!" she said to him.

"How would you know, if you haven't eaten the Fruit that givessss you that knowledge?"

He had a point. It was a classic Catch-22. For all she knew, the snake could be Good, and biting into the fruit could be a good thing. But until she bit the fruit, she wouldn't know.

Suddenly, the goat came walking by on its hind legs. This was the goat that had eaten of the Fruit. This was the goat that could walk upright, talk, and sing. This was the goat that Adam had named Phil Collins.

"I can feel it comin' in the air tonight," he sang.

"Oh, Lord," she said. "What should I do? It's just a fruit, after all. Why all the fuss? And look at what it did for the goat."

"Yessss," the snake hissed. "Look at what it did for the goat."

A fog rolled quickly in. Soon, all that was visible was the Tree, the Fruit, and the snake. What should she do? This was the land of confusion. Should she? Shouldn't she? Tree. Fruit. Snake. The only thing missing was God. The answer seemed obvious.

She took a bite. The fog rolled away.

"How isssss it?" the snake asked.

"Meh. It's all right, I guess," she said, and tossed the rest of the Fruit into a nearby bush, where it promptly caught fire.

"You'll regret this," came a voice from the bush.

"I guess?" she answered. "Honestly, I don't see what all the fuss was about. I don't seem any smarter, somehow. Calculus still eludes me as it did before. I'd eat more of it if I could learn calculus. Or even physics. Like the other day I dropped a pumpkin and a pea from the roof, and they hit the ground at the same time. That makes no sense to me still. Will I learn the answers to that?

"...Hello? Anything?"

The bush was done speaking. No reply at all.

6. That's a Lot of Trouble for a Pie

Evening had approached fast. The hut would have been enshrouded in darkness, had it not been for the little fiery pillars everywhere. She wasn't sure what they were, but they were trés romantic.

Adam looked at Eve. "Huh? Not bad, right?"

"It'll do," she understated.

"It'll do?"

"Just kidding. It's gorgeous."

"Well, you're my lady. And I wanna treat you right. After all, God said I could beat you whenever you get out of line, but He also said to cherish you. Which I find contradictory, but there you have it. I'm sure God won't make a habit of contradicting Himself."

"No," Eve agreed. "I'm sure He won't."

"Here, have some fermented juniper berries."

He poured a little in her Solo cup, and she took a sip. His face was instantaneously drenched in gin and saliva.

"No good?" he asked.

"No good? It's atrocious."

"Yeah, I think so too. But it can get you pretty hammered. That's why I keep it around."

"Typical male," she said.

"What the hell is that supposed to mean?"

"Not sure," she replied. "Anyway, do you have any of that fermented grape juice?"

"Wine?" he asked.

"Dooo youuu haave anny fermented graaape juiice?" she whined.

"No, I call it... ah, never mind. Here." He poured her a cup.

She sipped it. "Much better. So tell me, dear. What are these little tapered things on fire, and where did you find them?"

"Those are candles. And I found them at the most quaint dollar store."

"Really?" she asked.

"No, you ninny. I made them. From beeswax."

"What's beeswax?"

"Well, see, there are these things called bees that have built themselves a fine little home in the back garden. I haven't figured out the use for these creatures yet, as I have tried eating a dead one, and it didn't really taste much like anything, so I don't think it has much nutritional value. However, they do secrete the most amazing stuff that tastes absolutely wonderful in baking, or even made into a drink and fermented."

"Do you ferment everything?" she asked.

"Oh believe me," he said, with a wink. "I have tried."

"So what about the wax?" she asked, and was soon sorry she did.

"Well, unlike the honey, which they vomit from their stomachs, the wax is actually secreted from wax glands on their abdomen. It comes out in clear, tasteless, brittle flakes. The bees then chew and mold the shape into these series of hexagons. It takes over a thousand flakes to make one gram of wax (Source: Wikipedia). Each one of these candles weighs about a hundred grams, so that gives you some idea of how many bees it took to make the fifty or so candles you see here. Anyway, what I do is I put a chunk of the wax into a pot on the stove, melt it, pour it into a mold, then put what I call a wick in it, which is the thing that you see on fire, which I made out of hemp and sheep nut veins."

She looked at him from the corner of her eye.

"Yeah. It's exactly what it sounds like," clarified Adam. "Anyway, let's eat."

He walked over to an area of the hut that he called kitchen and grabbed some meat off what he called stove. He slapped down two pieces, one for Eve and one for himself, onto paper plates.

"What are these things you just put the meat on?" she asked.

"Those are paper plates. I made those too, by chopping down a tree and cutting the wood into chips, then I chemically separated the cellulose fibers into a pulp, pressed it and rolled it into a shape I call paper, then cut them into these shapes you see here called plates.

"Sounds like a lot of work," she said.

"Yes, but they save me from having to wash dishes."

He then scooped the side dishes onto the plates.

Eve ate ravenously. Although she'd sampled a few things from the garden, this was the first actual meal she'd had. And it was delicious.

"Wow," she said. "This is amazing. What are we eating?"

"Venison steaks from a deer I hunted, skinned, and butchered, then tossed in a pan with a little butter, garlic and rosemary, and whipped potatoes, and carrots that I sauteed in sage and brown butter."

"Marvelous."

"It's nothing, really. Anyone can cook if they get bored enough. I've had plenty of time to experiment, believe me."

"Which begs the question," said Eve, "How long have you been here?"

"I really don't know. A while. Time is such a relative thing, isn't it? Like, how do I even mark the passage of time, when nothing really changes? I mean, do I count the number of times the Sun has gone around the Earth? Do I use this here watch?"

Adam points to his wrist, and the black band around it; on the top, a digital display.

"Where did that come from?" Asked Eve.

"I haven't the foggiest. I'm not even sure what it does. I assume the numbers are supposed to measure time, but I'm not sure what each number means. Bah, no bother. I'll figure it out at some point I guess."

Before she knew it, she was done with her dinner.

"Now, who's ready for dessert?" Adam asked.

"No!" she shouted. "I want to live in the Garden with you. Please don't banish me to the desert. I've done nothing wrong."

"Not desert," Adam said. "Dessert. It's delicious and wonderful and it makes you feel... well, the opposite of how the desert would make you feel." He raced back to the kitchen and brought back a dish that was exuding the most intoxicating aroma. "Here. This is dessert."

"Sorry. I think it will take me a while to get used to the words you came up with to name things."

"It's all right. Perhaps I could have called this something else. The words do sound very similar. I suppose I could have called it pudding, like the British, but then what would I call actual pudding? Tell you what. I'll let you name this dish."

"Really?" she asked.

"Sure. Why not?"

"Terrific! I think I will name this... pie."

"Yeah, okay. That's the last time I'm going to let you name something."

"Why? I think pie is a cute word."

"Let me tell you a story. Out in the garden grows this tall, unassuming-looking grass that I call wheat. When the stalks look like they are starting to get heavy, I know it's time to harvest. I painstakingly separate each kernel from the stalk. I make sure there is no dirt or foreign materials left in the batch, and then I soak them to soften them up. Then I break up each kernel and separate what I call endosperm, for lack of a better term, from what I call bran. The bran makes me poop too much, but the animals seem to like it. The other stuff I turn into what I call flour. I then mix the flower with salt that I gathered from the mines a few miles away, sugar that I harvested from the cane, and butter which comes from a whole other process I'd rather not talk about. Then I roll it out into a sheet, fit it into this dish, and fill the middle with pears, raisins, cherries, and any other fruits that happen to be in season, as well as more sugar, this tree bark which I call cinnamon, as well as other spices that I have either plucked from a tree or bush, or from the ground. I bake it in an oven for quite some time, depending on how hot the fire is, trying to control the flame enough to cook thoroughly without burning it, and cut it with a hand-carved stone knife, and you wanna call it pie?"

"No good?"

7. Confession

Their first time making love was a strange jumble of tangled limbs, awkward fumbling, trying to find where things go, and a whole lot of messiness, and although we could have predicted all of that nonsense, Adam and Eve thought it would have gone much smoother. After all, God had created them with puzzle-piece parts, and it shouldn't have been that odd a trick to put them together. Once they got going, however, it was pure magic. It went on for quite some time, pushing, pulling, thrusting, retreating, over and over again, and just when they were beginning to tire of all of the nonsense, they both got the nice surprise at the end that makes rainbows and fireworks appear from out of nowhere.

Lying in bed in post-coital bliss, Eve's head a little delirious from all the spinning it had just done, her mouth started running before her brain had a chance to catch up. Women always have to ruin it by talking after. Adam, as we could have guessed, was sound asleep, snoring away. This began a long tradition of men doing the same thing for ages. This is why, to this day, we call it the Sleep of Adam. Huh? We don't? Well, then I hereby coin that phrase. Yes, you heard it here first, folks. So if anyone ever refers to a man's heavy sleep at the end of sex as the Sleep of Adam, remember, that's me.

"Adam?" she said.

Snore.

"Adam?" she said.

Snore.

"Adam??" she said, with a nudge of her elbow.

"Ngungg" he muttered.

"I have to say I underestimated you. Tonight. The candles. The most wonderful dinner. Making love. It was so romantic. You are so loving, so passionate, so caring. You know what I mean?"

"Nggrrrg," he muttered.

Sigh. "That's why I feel like I have to tell you something. I can't keep it a secret. We're partners, and partners share everything, right?"

"Ngrargh," he muttered.

"Well, I guess they do. I mean, we're the only partners I know. Human, anyway. But I've watched the animals, the ones who are monogamous, and they seem to share everything. So I suppose we should too, right?"

"Nrrrff," he muttered.

Sigh again. "All right, here goes. I ate the Forbidden Fruit."

"You what???" Adam's body sprang bolt upright in bed. A look entered his eyes that Eve couldn't distinguish between fear or anger. Perhaps it was both.

"I ate the Forbidden Fruit. Sorry..." she said, apprehensive.

He cradled his head in both hands. "Sorry. Sorry? My God, do you know what you've done?"

"Not really. It was just a bite. Nothing more than a nibble, really."

"It doesn't matter. God explicitly told us not to eat of the Fruit. Oh man, we're in deep doo-doo."

"Well, technically he told you. He never said anything to me about it."

"Have you forgotten that you are me, Riblet?"

"Only by a technicality. I'm my own person, too."

"Obviously not, since you can't even make proper decisions for yourself."

"Sorry..."

"Sorry. Sorry."

"Yes, Adam. I'm very sorry. I don't know what else to say."

"Well, you better think of something," said Adam.

"We don't even know what this means. Maybe nothing will happen."

"This could be the end of the world as we know it."

"I feel fine," she said. "Nothing has changed. I don't feel any smarter. I don't feel like I know anything I didn't before. Some Tree of Knowledge. What is he doing testing us with Fruit, anyway? He knows all there is to do in this life is eat, sleep, and poop. Eventually, we were going to try that Fruit. Why would he put it there just to tempt us? It makes no sense."

Adam glared.

"So I failed a test. Big deal. I'm sure this will just be one of many tests we'll fail in our lifetime. We're allowed mistakes." She looked at Adam. "Aren't we?"

He shook his head. "I don't know. I don't think so."

"Well, that's insane. I mean, we're only human."

"What is that supposed to mean?"

"I don't know. I just think that maybe it's part of the human condition. We're given free will. We can do as we choose. Therefore, it only goes to follow that we're going to make some mistakes."

"This," Adam said, "was not a mistake. This was disobedience, plain and simple. We're going to be in so much trouble. Go to sleep. We'll talk about this in the morning."

It was difficult for Adam to get back to sleep, knowing all the possible punishments that God had in store, but the Sleep of Adam (I really think that's a winner) soon overcame him, and he was out.

Some time passed, but not enough, before Eve started running her yapper again.

"Adam?"

"Ngerrrrgh!"

"I just had a thought. I was thinking that it would be a much nicer life if I could let myself live in the now a little more. Then I realized that everything we see travels at the speed of light and is not instantaneous. Therefore, everything we think we're experiencing now is actually in the past. Pretty cool, huh? Or is that depressing? Maybe this Fruit is working after all.

"Phlrrrp."

"Adam?"

"Mmmmm?"

"Tomorrow, will you go out to the garden with me and take a bite of the Fruit? I mean, we have nothing to lose at this point. I already messed things up. I just think we should do everything together. Isn't that what couples do? They do everything together? I mean, I don't know what humans are supposed to do, but I noticed that the sheep and goats, they do everything together. Will you please take a bite of the Fruit for me? Please?"

"Oh my God, woman!" Adam blasphemed. "Fine! I will take a bite, now for the love of God, will you please let me get some sleep?"

"Sure," Eve giggled. "Good night," she said.

"You mean good morning." Adam looked at the digital numbers on his watch. "I think."

8. Eden's End

They stood there, hand in hand, at the foot of the Tree. The core that she had tossed on the ground had long since vanished, most likely eaten by that very intelligent goat.

"I'm nervous," Adam said.

"Don't be. Like I said, I already ate the Fruit. Whatever damage there was is done. You may as well grab one and take a bite and get it over with."

"But what if I can be saved? I mean, it's you that took the bite, innit? Maybe you'll be the one punished, and I'll be okay. My record's clean. I mean, it'll suck to lose you, but I do have more ribs, so..."

A slap landed across his face. "How dare you!" she shouted.

"No good?"

"No. No good. As you said, we are one. What happens to me happens to you. And how can you even think about loving another rib?"

"Yes, dear. I'm sorry, dear," he said, plucking a Fruit from the Tree.

Phil Collins the goat walks by once again. "I can feel it coming in the air tonight," he sang again.

"Oh Lord," Eve said. "He sang that before."

"Yeah, he likes that song," said Adam. "Especially at ominous times like these."

STOP! A voice came from above.

"Say wha?" Adam asked.

DO NOT, I REPEAT, DO NOT, EAT OF THIS FRUIT!

Adam and Eve looked at each other. "God," they both said.

"Listen, God," began Adam. "I appreciate everything you've done for me thus far. Really. I do. But what's the deal with this Tree? Why would you put it here just to tempt us? Seems kind of cruel, dunnit?"

I AM THE GOD OF THE OLD TESTAMENT. AND I AM CRUEL! (It's not till Jesus that I decide to tone it down a bit.) NOW, DO AS I SAY! (Although, it is your choice.)

"So, can you please answer me what the deal is with this Tree?"

THIS IS THE TREE OF KNOWLEDGE. IF YOU EAT OF THE FRUIT YOU'LL...KNOW THINGS.

"Oh yeah? Like what kind of things?" Adam asked, although he already knew the answer.

LIKE GOOD AND EVIL. YOU'LL KNOW IF THE THINGS YOU DO ARE BAD OR GOOD!

"Forgive me for asking, dear Lord, but don't we want to know those things? Don't you want us to do good?"

YES! YOU BETTER BE GOOD, FOR GOODNESS SAKE! BUT I DON'T WANT YOU TO KNOW THAT THE THING YOU'RE DOING IS GOOD UNTIL I TELL YOU THAT IT'S GOOD, AND ONLY THEN CAN I...OH, TO HELL WITH IT. I'M GOD! DON'T QUESTION MY METHODS! YOU KNOW, THE WHOLE MYSTERIOUS WAYS AND ALL THAT.

"Then why did the snake ask me to eat the Fruit?" Eve asked.

I'M SORRY, IS SHE TALKING?

"Rude," said Eve.

"Then why did the snake ask her to eat the Fruit?" Adam repeated.

THE SNAKE WAS SENT FROM THE DARKNESS. IT WAS EVIL PERSONIFIED... SNAKE-IFIED.

"Aha!" Eve said. "How was I supposed to know that if I hadn't eaten the Fruit?"

YEAH, CAN WE GET AN INTERPRETER HERE?

"Hey! Rude!" said Eve again.

"How was she supposed to know the snake was evil if she hadn't eaten the Fruit? Don't you see? It's a Catch-22!"

JOSEPH HELLER. GOOD BOOK. ALTHOUGH I DON'T QUITE CARE FOR THE NAME OF THE AUTHOR. LISTEN, I HAVE STUFF TO DO, LIKE REST. DO WHAT YOU WANT. YOU HAVE FREE WILL. GOOD-BYE.

"So, did he really mean do what we want?" asked Adam.

"Just take a bite.," said Eve.

Adam took a rather large bite.

"You know," he said, with his mouth full of food, "Maybe we're not the only intelligent species out there."

"Didn't I tell you? Instant brains!" said Eve.

"Hmm. Maybe you shouldn't eat any more of this Fruit. We don't want you becoming too smart. After all, what good is an intelligent woman?"

"Ugh. Men are pigs!" she shouted, and stormed off.

"Kidding!" he shouted back at her, and tossed the half-eaten Fruit.

Adam stood there watching, mouth agape, as the Fruit struck the ground with the force of a meteorite, smashing through the surface of the planet and creating a sucking vacuum that pulled Adam and Eve down through and out of the Garden of Eden forever.

9. Gifts from Heaven

Adam awoke to find himself in the middle of a desolate landscape. His head was pounding. To his left lay Eve, still as the air around him.

"Eve?" he said. No response.

"Eve??" he said, a little more urgently. Still nothing.

He put his ear up to her mouth. No breath. She was dead. At least, he thought that's what that meant. He rolled her over onto her back. If she wasn't going to breathe, then he would shove his breath into her mouth hole until she had enough that she could do it on her own. He forced all the air in his own lungs into hers. Nothing. He did it again. Nothing. One more time. Her chest remained still. Perhaps if he pressed up and down on her chest, maybe then it would start moving. He did it once, twice, three times. Stayin' alive...stayin' alive. The phrase was repeating over and over in his head rhythmically. He breathed into her mouth again, compressed her chest again, alternating back and forth until, success! Her open eyes focused on Adam and she smiled.

"Eve! You're alive! See, God? You're not the only one who can do it. I gave her life, too!"

Her smile turned to worry as she got a look at the desert all around her. "Where are we?" she asked.

"I don't know. But this definitely isn't Eden anymore."

Incidentally, they were in Mesopotamia, otherwise known as Iraq. Oddly enough, it wasn't much different from modern-day Iraq.

"I told you I didn't want to be banished to the desert!" she shouted. "Bring me back to the Garden!"

"I didn't do this, Eve."

"Why? Why did you bring us here?"

"You gotta believe me, sweetie. I didn't bring us here. I have no idea where we are, or how we got here."

"We're gonna die!" she yelled. "We're gonna die out here in the desert!"

Adam grabbed he by the shoulders. "Eve, listen to me. Calm down. You gotta keep your wits. Strange things happen all the time in my life. I'm used to it by now. Everything is a new experience. This is just another new experience. I'll get through this like I've gotten through everything. We'll get through this. We'll find our way back, I'm sure of it. And if not, we'll have to make the best of this."

"Easy for you to say," said Eve.

"Maybe. Life has been pretty easy thus far. Why should I expect any different? You know dear, this could be the start of something WATCH OUT!"

Adam shoved her out of the way, to just barely avoid being hit by a large colorful object falling from the sky. It hit the ground with a loud Whumph!

"What in the world is that?" asked Eve.

"Looks like some sort of gift."

It was. A gift, standing about four feet tall, wrapped in snowman wrapping paper, all done up with a large red bow.

"Who's it from?" she asked. "There's no tag on it."

"Hmm. Oh, wait. There's a card."

"Open it, open it!!" she said a little too enthusiastically, given their situation.

"All right, I'm getting to it."

THE ALPHABET BOOKS: ABC

Inside the envelope was a very tasteful card. On the front was a picture of a fat man in a sleigh being pulled through the air by eight caribou. Happy Holidays it said, written in glittery font. He opened it up. "May Your Days Be Merry and Bright!" it said on the inside. A little too generic, if you ask me. Handwritten on the opposite page was a note. It was from you-know-who.

"He even writes in all caps," said Adam. "Jeesh."

DEAR ADAM AND EVE,
YOU HAVE DISOBEYED ME FOR THE FIRST AND LAST TIME. I GAVE YOU FREE WILL, SO I GUESS A LITTLE OF THIS IS ON MY SHOULDERS. HOWEVER, YOU NEED TO KNOW THAT YOUR ACTIONS HAVE CONSEQUENCES. I'M SORRY IF THIS IS A VERY HARSH PUNISHMENT, BUT AS YOU KNOW, I AM A VERY CRUEL AND UNFORGIVING GOD. FOR NOW. IN THOUSANDS OF YEARS I MAY LIGHTEN UP A LITTLE. SINCE YOU NOW KNOW THE DIFFERENCE BETWEEN GOOD AND EVIL, IT IS MY DUTY TO INFORM YOU THAT YOU HAVE CREATED A GRAVE SIN BY EATING OF THE FRUIT. YOUR PUNISHMENTS ARE AS FOLLOWS:

YOU ARE TO LIVE IN THE DESERT. NO MORE WILL YOU BE ABLE TO VISIT THE GARDEN THAT I SO LOVINGLY CREATED FOR YOU. IT HAS SINCE BEEN DEMOLISHED TO MAKE WAY FOR LUXURY CONDOS.

ADAM, YOU WILL NO LONGER BE PROVIDED WITH FREE FOOD. YOU WILL HAVE TO TILL THE LAND AND GROW VEGETATION BY YOURSELF. I HAVE LEFT YOU YOUR GOAT, SO THAT YOU

MAY EAT OF ITS FLESH IF YOU WISH AND GET MILK, ALTHOUGH IT WILL BE DIFFICULT TO DO, SINCE PHIL COLLINS IS A MALE GOAT. WHATEVER MILK YOU ARE ABLE TO SQUEEZE FROM HIM IS PROBABLY NOT MILK, SO I WOULDN'T DRINK IT IF I WERE YOU.

EVE, YOUR LOVE-MAKING SESSION FROM THE OTHER NIGHT HAS PRODUCED A CHILD INSIDE OF YOUR BODY. IN THE WEEKS TO COME, YOU WILL KNOW THE HORRIBLE PAIN THAT IS CHILDBIRTH.

YOU ARE NO LONGER PURE. YOU NOW KNOW OF THE DIFFERENCE BETWEEN GOOD AND EVIL, AND YOU WILL BE FOREVER LABELED AS SINNERS. AS FURTHER CONSEQUENCE, EVERY CHILD BORN AFTERWARD WILL HAVE SIN BORN INTO THEM. YOUR CHILDREN WILL BE RIGHT LITTLE BASTARDS, THEY WILL. GOOD LUCK WITH THEM.

INSIDE THE PACKAGE IS THE AFOREMENTIONED GOAT, SOME GARDENING EQUIPMENT, AS WELL AS A VARIETY OF SEEDS TO PRODUCE NUMEROUS FRUITS AND VEGETABLES. I MADE SURE TO LEAVE YOU PLENTY OF FORBIDDEN FRUIT SEEDS, SINCE YOU SEEM TO LIKE THEM SO MUCH.

TAKE CARE,

G.

"Hmm," Adam said. "Well, that sucks."

"Yeah," Eve agreed.

"Now look," said Adam, "I'm not going to blame anyone, but it seriously is all your fault that we're here."

"I accept that," she said, not arguing like Adam expected. He realized that this would be one of the few times in history that this would happen, so he figured he'd better not push it by elaborating on just how badly she screwed them both.

"I'm sorry. Really I am. Listen, let's go see if we can find a spot to make shelter and we'll figure out what we're going to do from there, okay?"

He dried her tears with his hand as she nodded.

"Hold on a minute, Eve. You have something in your ear."

"Baaah, get it out get it out!!" she screamed.

"Okay, I will, just calm down. Look, it's a twig. Huh. You must have gotten tangled in the bush before your fault. Fault? Did I say your fault? I meant your fall. Haha. Hey, good thing you didn't land in the burning bush. You would probably still be on fire right now."

"What was up with that bush, anyway? Always burning, never burnt. That's not how chemistry is supposed to work." Tears came in a river down her cheeks.

"Aww, what's wrong?" he asked.

"You know," she said, after her tears dried up and she was able to speak, "I'm gonna miss the weirdness. Nothing there made sense, but it was home, you know? Now we get this...this...this nowhere to live in. This plain, boring nowhere."

"Meh. It may be nowhere, but I would say it's anything but boring. Presents falling from the sky. We still have Phil Collins, the talking goat. I have a feeling things will be pretty interesting around here. And don't think of it as a desert. Think of it as a beach. Now, don't just stand there. Help me unwrap this package."

10. Seeds

They unwrapped the gift together. Beneath the snowman wrapping paper was a plain cardboard box. Although neither of them had seen cardboard before, Adam was already turning ideas over in his head as to how he could make it. He was pretty sure that it wasn't that much different than the paper plates he had made.

"Well," Adam said as he looked over at Eve, "Here goes."

God hadn't bothered taping the box, which was just as well, because Adam probably would have been more occupied with the novelty of the tape than what was inside the box. God had instead, folded flap over flap, in the Escher-style that we all know how to do when there is no tape. This was convenient for God, but not so convenient for Adam, as he was now fully occupied with the novelty of the fold.

"Look at this, Eve. Look at how God folded the flaps. It's like a never-ending staircase."

"Yeah, I'm not really sure what that is." As the world had yet to become crowded, and the concept of family had yet to be invented, there was never any need to build any other levels, hence, no staircases.

Adam, who had dreamed of staircases, tried to explain. "Staircase, you know...Uh, like a ladder, kinda, but...umm...different. Kinda."

"Sure," Eve said. "Well, let's open this." She put her

hand under one flap and was stopped by Adam. "Wait. Just take a second and look at this. Don't you see? You follow the flaps to the left, they go up, up, up forever. Follow them to the right and they go forever down. I bet if I found a perfectly round rock and put it on one of the flaps, it would just go to the right, down forever. This is incredible. Only God could create something like this."

"Yeah, no. Look," said Eve, as she unfolded the flaps and refolded them, over and over.

Adam's eyes widened. "That's magic!" he said. "Witch!"

Eve laughed. "No, I'm not a witch, dude. If you look closely you'll notice that the flaps all rise slightly even though it looks like..."

"Yep. Okay," Interrupted Adam. "Hey, let's see what's inside!"

Inside the box was another box. And inside that one, another box.

"Ahh, God," said Adam. "Ever the trickster. Good one."

The third box had been partially chewed through.

"Phil Collins!" Adam shouted excitedly.

"About damn time," Phil Collins said. "I thought you guys would be standing there chit-chatting all day. Thought I would starve to death in there; I was about to eat all these seeds."

"Yeah, let's see what we got," said Eve.

"Wow, look at all this," said Adam. "We got a diggy thing, a little claw thing, a thing with a pointy thing on it. Another flat thing with a wobbly thing. A thing with a thing under it. And, ooh, look at this thing. Ooh, we got seeds, look at all the seeds we got. Lemmesee, we got pumpkin seeds, pear seeds, tomato seeds, wow there must be hundreds of different varieties of seeds here. God hooked us up. See? He doesn't hate us. We got it pretty good here."

"This is a joke. Don't you get it? We have all these seeds to plant, and nowhere to plant them. Just miles and miles of sand. Plants need water. Where is the water? How the hell is anything going to grow in this? God hooked us up? No, God set us up. We're going to die out here, Adam. We're going to starve to death."

"Nah, we'll be all right," Adam said.

"I don't know how you can be so positive right now."

"Because being negative is a waste of time. It's not productive at all. And it's not realistic. Things have a way of working themselves out for me. Always. I was feeling lonely, you appeared one day. I was tiring of the boring selection of fruits and vegetables, God showed me the way to other delicious ones. He provides."

Eve laughed. So hard. "You idiot."

"What?"

"God doesn't provide. He doesn't watch out for us. Not any more. God abandoned us. He's gone. This box was his parting gift. There is no more God."

"That doesn't make sense, Eve. You can't get rid of God. He is there all the time. Like our breath and our heartbeat."

"Which will also leave us, at some point."

"Oh, Eve. Always so full of negativity."

"Really?" Eve asked. "Really, Adam? Here. We should really have saved this for when we got hungry, but here. You need this." She kicked the sand away from a fallen Forbidden Fruit, that had gotten sucked down into the abyss with them.

"I'm not really..."

"Eat. It has nothing to do with hunger. You need to

see for yourself."

"Well, okay," said Adam.

And the more he ate, the more the dumb optimistic expression left his face. The Fruit was allowing the understanding to seep its way into his brain

"You see?" she asked. "You getting it now?"

"No," said Adam. "No, no, no. It can't be. Eve? God is dead, isn't he?"

"Yeah. He is. To us, anyway. This is it, Adam. It's just you and me and Phil Collins until we die of starvation in this awful place."

"Phil? Say it ain't so, Phil!" Adam pleaded.

Phil shook his head. "Listen. You know I love you, but I just can't take this," he said, and walked away.

"Phil, come back!" Adam shouted.

And Phil would come back. Even though he was a thousand times smarter than Adam, he still needed time to process all of this.

11. Sometimes You Gotta Make Do

Life in the desert turned out to be not so bad after all.

Their home wasn't anything that would appear in any magazines, for sure, but it was cozy, and protected them from the blazing sun. They had to travel far for water, and even when they found little pools here and there, they were usually quite tiny. They had to use the water for drinking purposes only, both for Adam and Eve as well as Phil Collins. So the water that glued the sand together to make the mud for their hut wasn't made of water, but rather the byproduct of water that happens after it flows through the digestive system. Stink? A little. But after the sun had baked all of the impurities out of the urine-coated sand, the smell was no longer there, and they were left with a very sturdy hut that stood up fairly well against the hot desert winds.

Growing produce had been a bit of a struggle, and at times Adam got to thinking that maybe he should change what he named produce to nonproduce. It didn't have that much of a ring to it, however, so he decided to keep the old term and keep hoping for the best.

Digging through the sand hadn't been much of a challenge; it was finding the right spots to dig in. They needed to be damp spots, which, as I have said, were few and far between. He could only plant a few seeds near each oasis he had found, for he didn't want the plants to suck up the only water there was. They needed to make sure they had enough for their own bodies to hydrate with.

It was an entire year before the first tree bore any fruit. And what a difficult year that had been. The water pools had gotten to be tens of miles away, and by the time he reached them, he had to drink half of it just to have enough strength to make it to the next one. For food, luckily the occasional desert rat would scurry by, and he would roast it over an open fire. On very rare occasions, a camel or something would get close enough so that Adam could slaughter it. By the end of the year, Adam had gotten pretty good at hunting camel, keeping alert enough for any sign of movement despite the hallucinations he had been having that were brought on by dehydration in the searing heat. Camels weren't that difficult to catch, as they weren't what you'd exactly call fast, but tracking them was a whole different matter. Sure, they left footprints in the sand, which were rare indeed, but any time the desert breeze would blow, it would just cover them back up. The good thing is, once an animal was killed, the meat would dry in seconds, so it would keep for quite some time. The bad news is, the meat would dry in seconds, so there was very little water content in it; far from enough for them to stay hydrated.

So it was exactly one year later (although Adam was terrible at telling the passage of time, out here where there were no seasons made it particularly difficult) when the first Fruit blossomed on a Knowledge Tree. These were the first plants to sprout any food, so for a while, both breakfast and dinner consisted of camel-wrapped Knowledge Fruit. At first it was pretty good. The camel meat had added a certain gaminess that had been lacking in the Fruit thus far. After a while, they became tired of the taste, but they were always grateful that these were the first fruits to blossom. The more they ate, the smarter they became. The smarter they became, the more new and innovative ways Adam was inventing to grown more food. And so on.

Luckily it was only a few months before other things began to produce food, and soon Adam had quite the garden growing. Although it couldn't technically be called a garden. Eden was a garden. This was more like scattered plants. But no matter. He had drawn a little map to where each plant was, and soon he knew the layout like he knew Eve's body, and didn't need a map anymore. Eve, having been disappointed at their love-making sessions from time to time, had wished that he had made a map of her body. But I digress. The point is, soon they were almost as comfortable there as they had been in Eden, and the beauty of it was, both Adam and Eve had made it with their own hands this time. This gave them a greater appreciation for what they had. Every time Adam looked at his surroundings (as barren as they were), his home, his gardens, everything was because of what they did. (He had very quickly forgotten that God had given them the seeds and the tools to till the land in the first place, but really, who's keeping score?)

Soon they were eating like kings. Adam had invented some pretty cool cooking devices, from the first self-cleaning oven to the first microwave. His testicles tingled every time he used it, but it cooked things in seconds. He didn't really know why he wanted things to cook so quickly, since they had nothing but time there, and often after meals they would just sit around and stare at each other with nothing to do.

All this staring led to boredom, which led to the invention of games. Tic-Tac-Toe, backgammon, pin the tail on Phil Collins. They had to get Phil pretty wasted on wine before they played, as they used very sharp vulture bones to fasten the camel tail to his rear end. Phil had been a pretty good sport about the whole thing, oddly enough. The wine made him forget that he was stuck here with these yahoos for eternity.

12. Belly

"Hold still," Eve said to Adam, and reached into his ear.

"Ow! What the..." he said, as it felt like whatever she was pulling from his ear was attached to his brain stem. Every nerve, from his neck up through his sinuses, shot up with an electric charge, and he sneezed.

"Huh. Look at this," she said, and showed him the twig she pulled from his ear.

"That's weird," replied Adam. "Remember the time when you had one in your ear?"

"No," she said.

"It was right after we had landed here from Eden."

"Don't remember."

"I'm not surprised. You were pretty dazed," said Adam. "Anyway, honey? If I say something, do you promise not to get mad?"

"No," she replied.

"No you won't get mad, or no you won't promise to not get mad?"

"The last one."

"Okay. Never mind then."

"Oh no," she said. "You can't do that."

"Do what?"

"You can't start something off by asking me not to get mad, then not tell me what you didn't want me to get mad about. Just spill it. I won't get mad. I promise."

"Now you're just saying that because you want me to tell you what I was going to tell you."

"Yes. I am. Now tell me."

He took a deep breath. "All right. Here goes. Now, don't take this the wrong way."

"..."

"You know, I love your body, right? I mean, your soft shoulders, your legs, your...you know."

Her eyes rolled. "Get to the point."

"It's, um, your belly. I mean, don't get me wrong. I love your belly. Love it. It's just, well, it's gotten, um, a little, um, big."

He braced himself for the punch to his jaw, but it never came. Instead, she sighed and dropped her shoulders in a melancholy fashion. "I know," she said. "I'm not sure what's going on."

"How much have you been eating?" he asked.

"You should know. We eat all of our meals together." She then added, softly, "Except for the ones I sneak."

"You're sneaking meals?" he asked. "No wonder you're getting fat! Honey, you can't do that. We only have so much food to go around."

"I'm sorry. Really. I'm just always so hungry. Even right after we eat a meal, I'm still starving. It's as if I'm eating for two people."

Adam's head quickly swiveled and his eyes grew big. "Wait, what did you just say?"

"I'm sorry. Really. I'm just always so hungry. Even right after we eat a meal, I'm still starving. It's as if I'm eating for two people."

"That's it!" he shouted.

"What's it?"

"Don't you get it? You feel like you're eating for two

people because you are eating for two people. There's a person in there." He pointed at her stomach.

"A person?" she asked. "Are you sure?"

"Sure I'm sure. It only makes sense."

"Yeah. It makes sense to me too. You know, once in a while I can feel it moving around in there. I thought it was really bad indigestion. But just yesterday I thought I saw an outline of a foot underneath my belly skin. Well, that's solved, I guess..." A look of fear entered her face rather quickly. "Wait, what? A person? Oh no. No! What do I do? Get it out! Get it out!"

"I can't."

"Why not?"

"What do you want me to do, rip you open?"

"Yes! If you have to," she said.

"I don't think I have to. Look, remember in God's Christmas card he sent, he told you that you would have to experience the pain of childbirth?"

"Unfortunately."

"I think you're going to have to experience the pain of childbirth."

"Which means?"

"Which means it'll probably come out on its own."

"How?"

"The way I see it, there is one of two ways. It's in your stomach, right? You know how food comes out, once it's digested?"

"Oh no. No way."

"Yeah. It'll come out like poop comes out."

Adam smiled.

"What have you got to smile about?"

"Poop. Still one of my favorite words I invented. Always makes me smile."

"Adam, focus."

"All right, so anyway, yeah it may come out that way."

"Kill me now," she said.

"You'll be fine."

"Easy for you to say. Ouch, that's gonna rip me a new one."

"Heh. Yeah, probably."

"Wait, you said one of two ways. What's the other way?"

"Well, you remember how we created the baby?"

"No."

"No clue?"

"No. It just started happening all of a sudden. One day I noticed my belly had started getting big. And before I knew it, it was moving."

"God's note said it was from our lovemaking session."

"We're never doing that again," she said.

"Haha, we'll see."

"No, I'm serious, Adam. We are never ever doing that again."

"Baby, you know you can't resist this."

"Try me," said Eve. "So anyway, you think it could come out of there?"

"Seems logical enough," Adam said.

"While that doesn't seem quite as bad, it still seems like it's going to hurt. Like, a lot."

"Meh," said Adam. "Nonsense. I fit in there just fine. I'm sure it will be a piece of cake."

"You fit in there just fine, all right," she agreed. "Your teeny little codpiece, anyway. Not your entire body."

"Hey, my codpiece is not teeny."

"It is compared to a whole person!" she answered.

"Fair enough."

"Yeah."

"I don't think it'll be all that bad, you know. I mean, how big can this person actually be? It's small enough to fit in your stomach, right? What can it be, all of five pounds? Six at most? You'll be okay. Why, my codpiece must weigh at least four and a half."

"Dream on," she said, and with that, the conversation dropped, and soon, they forgot about the person growing inside of her for a while.

Until...

13. What Is Wrong with These Kids Today?

Cain was born a little prematurely, so his birth weight was less than four pounds. However, his size was a poor predictor of his temperament, as he had the piss-poor attitude of a rhinoceros charging down a runway full of wounded peacocks. God said it would happen, and it did. Not only could the little bastard not take care of himself, he was absolutely worthless. He had no worth. He was a total waste of space. A little space, true, but a waste nonetheless. He never ate his vegetables, he ran around the house all crazy, tracking mud outdoors, vivisected defenseless animals while they were still alive, and he would always knock pictures off the wall. What a little asshole. Fuck.

Whew. I apologize for my language, but wow, what a prick.

"You know," Adam began, "I was thinking...Ow!"

"Sorry, honey. You had a really big eyebrow hair that was bugging the hell out of me."

"You couldn't have waited? I was thinking."

"Yeah, but look at this," she said, and showed him the hair she had just plucked.

"What the...?"

"Looks like a twig," she said.

"I know. Looks like the same thing we've been finding growing out of our ears lately. What do you think is going on?"

"I don't know. Must be the desert heat making our hair grow thicker or something."

"Don't you think the opposite should happen? Shouldn't our hair grow thinner instead?"

"Careful, Adam. You're treading too close to Natural Selection territory."

"Anyway, as I was saying, I was thinking. I may have a way we can get back into God's good graces and get back into Eden."

"Why? Do you not like it here? Hahaha," she said, sarcastically.

"Hahaha. As fun as this is, I want Eden back." He looked around as if someone else were listening. "I mean, I would really like to get right with the Lord," he said, then whispered to Eve, "I really want Eden back."

"Okay, so what's your plan?" she asked.

"I think we should really show Him just how sorry we are. Let's jump in the river."

"Not now, Adam. Tell me what your penance idea is."

"We should jump in the river."

"Fine, but then will you tell me what your idea of penance is?"

"That's it. We get in the river."

"That's the punishment? How is that punishment?"

"We'll stay there for forty-seven days."

"Why forty-seven?" she asked.

"Why not forty-seven?"

"Right now, I would hang out in a river for a thousand days. I am so tired of this heat it'll be a welcome relief. I still don't see how that's penance."

"Don't you? We'll get all pruney."

"But where do we find a river around here?" she asked.

"That's the good news. There's one closer than we

thought. The Tigris is only a couple days' trek away."

"The Tigris? Isn't that, like, icy cold?"

"It's a little chilly, yeah. But this is penance. Get it now?"

"Jeez, I guess so now. We'll die before the first hour's up."

"Maybe. But look at it this way, water problem's solved."

"Great. Where did you come up with this idea?"

"I had a vision."

"You had a vision. Well, that's nice. Did your vision include you dying of hypothermia?"

"Well...see that's the thing. I'll be in another river."

"What? Another river? Why another river?"

"It's just, I think part of our penance should be spending time away from each other. Solitude, you know? Nobody likes being alone. I think it'll make for lots of brownie points with the Big Guy."

"Fine, where you gonna go? Euphrates?"

"Jordan," he answered.

"Jordan?" blurted Eve. "Jordan? Are you kidding me?"

"What?" he asked.

"I suppose you're going to one of those all-inclusive resorts. Gonna lounge by the pool and drink some daiquiris?"

"What are you talking about?" asked Adam. "I'll be immersed in the river for forty-seven days. Just like you."

"Oh, poor you. Bathing in room temperature waters while I'm freezing my butt off. That's nice."

"Listen, it's not gonna be a picnic for me either. I have to walk for weeks through the desert to get there."

Her eyebrows arched, causing a twig-hair to go schproiiinnngg!

"Well, okay. I'm hitching a ride on Phil Collins."

"You're going to sit on Phil Collins the whole way through the desert? You'll break him! How does he feel about this?"

"I'm on my way; I'm making it," Phil sang.

"See? He's on is way. He's making it." Adam added, "That's a new song for you, Phil. Where did you learn this little ditty?"

"A little angel named Gabriel," he answered.

"See? I'll be okay. You'll be okay."

"I'll be freezing my ass off," she reminded him.

"Fine then. You know what? You only have to stay there for forty days. How's that? I'll stay in my river for forty-seven, you stay for forty."

"What do we do about the little asshole?" Eve asked.

"Cain? Leave him. That's another side bonus. A vacation from him for a month or so. What do you think about that?" he asked.

"Which way's the river?" she replied.

14. Tigris

It did take a couple days for Eve to make the trek across the desert to the Tigris. With every other step she cursed Adam's name. As she sat by the bank of the icy river, dipping her toe in the water, she cursed his name loudly. Screamed it, in fact. She knew the water was going to be cold, but the actual feel of it on her skin brought a whole new meaning to the word.

"Oh, Adam, why did I let you talk me into this?" she asked. "Curse you, Adam! And curse your name!" she shouted into the sky, which caused a dozen birds that had been lounging along the river to fly directly up, sending down in return a bright white beam of light.

"Huh?" asked Eve dumbly, as out of the bright light there appeared a beautiful figure. An angel, most would have thought. And yes, it was an angel, but this angel had a mean streak and a penchant for mischief. Due to the knowledge she had gained from eating the Fruits, she knew right away that this was Satan himself. He approached her slowly, with gentility and grace, and placed a hand on her shoulder.

"Dear child," he said. "You don't have to do this."

"What do you mean?" asked Eve. "Of course I do."

"Why?" asked Satan. "Because Adam said so?"

"Well, yeah. I mean, I guess. He is the man of the house, after all."

"Man of the house?" Satan said. "Would a man make

his woman spend forty days in freezing cold water while he lives in luxury in the golden waters of the Jordan?"

"Well, I..."

"Would a man not invite his wife to come join him in those golden waters, rather than send her away?"

"You know, I..."

"Or at the very least, would a man not come join his wife in the icy waters, rather than forcing her to endure the pain alone?"

"Hmm, you know, you have a point."

"Of course I have a point. He's making you do the penance while he does nothing. It won't work. God won't forgive either of you this way. His was a dumb idea."

"Perhaps," she said. "But how do you know God won't forgive me at least?"

"Because," Satan said, with a smile, "God doesn't forgive. He banished you to here because you ate a Fruit? One that you had no idea how good or bad it was, because you hadn't eaten the Fruit yet? Does that make sense?"

"No, I suppose not."

"And get this. God told me I had to worship Adam. Not sure what that's all about. I asked God, isn't it enough to worship You, I have to worship this guy too? He's just a person. He doesn't need to be worshiped."

"And what did God say?"

"He said that Adam was made in His image, and that he was an extension of God himself. I then asked Him, wouldn't that be worshiping a false idol? Isn't that a sin?"

"What did God say?"

"He told me to quit arguing and get out of His face. So here I am."

"God kicked you out of Heaven?"

"Apparently."

"For how long?"

"I don't know. For good, I guess?"

"Is there nothing you can do to get back?" she asked.

"I don't know. But it sure as hell isn't standing in this cold river. God doesn't care about that. I don't wanna go back, anyway."

"Where will you go?" she asked. "You can't stay on Earth. You'll lose your angel status."

"There's a place that's far sweeter than Heaven. And it's down below."

"You mean Hell?"

"It's not as bad as everyone makes it out to be. Besides, as soon as I enter Hell's gates, the place will be that much cooler. Everyone already likes me down there." He looked at his watch. "Listen, I gotta go. Just remember what I said about Adam. He ain't shit. Look at the child he gave you. If he was so great, don't you think he could've produced something better than that Cain kid? Anyway, do what you want; it's your life. I just wouldn't get in that river if I were you. Laters."

And just as quickly as he came, he was gone.

That's it, thought Eve, I'm packing up and going home.

15. Meanwhile, on the Left Bank...

Adam sat on the edge of the river in a lounge chair, daiquiri in his hand. Okay, maybe he wasn't actually in the river, but he was near the river, and he did take occasional dips in the water anytime he wanted to cool off a little (or do penance. Ahem). He had gathered quite the audience of animals; little birds and deer followed him around wherever he strolled. He felt like Jesus would feel in his heyday. None of this was natural; they were all instructed by God to follow him around and worship him. There wasn't one creature in the bunch that thought Adam was worth much as a human, never mind an entity that needed to be worshiped. But what could they do but follow God's orders? They really hadn't any say in the matter. If they all did what God said, perhaps they would be in a better place when they died. It never occurred to any of them that they had no souls, and they weren't going anywhere.

"Get me another drink, will ya Phil?" Adam asked, and if goats had fingers, boy, Phil would sure have used one of them right then.

Phil poured him a drink from the blender, as he took another dip in the Jordan. The water was so nice! It actually was quite fantastic here; perhaps he could convince Eve to move out here with him. It did suck that he had to walk all the way back to Iraq to ask her, then turn around and walk all the way back here. It was then that Adam's relaxed mind had fallen asleep, dreaming about some future time when the telephone would be invented.

Before he could drown, he was startled awake by a couple of dolphins passing a beach ball back and forth. For a minute, they debated letting him drown, since they didn't really care much for Adam, but they needed a human to throw the ball, and he would do in a pinch.

"Oh, hey Chip. Hey Dale. Thanks for stopping by. Here ya go," he said, and bopped the ball high in the air. Chip flicked the ball with his tail, to Dale, who caught it on his nose, and they swam away. "Bye guys!" he shouted at them.

Forty seven days had passed of this nonsense, and it was time to head on back home. All he could hope was God was witnessing what a sacrifice he was making, and that he would get back into His good graces. It would certainly be a shame if he holy fuck what was that on his shoulder? It looked like a peeling flap of skin, but it had a very dry, hard, yet brittle consistency. It almost resembled the bark of a tree. Skin shouldn't be like that. "Ouch!" he yelped as he plucked it off. It hurt quite badly, doing that, and he watched for blood. There was no blood to follow, however, there was a clear fluid oozing from his shoulder that had the consistency of sap.

Odd, he thought. Now where was I.. Oh yeah. It would certainly be a shame if he had walked all this way and endured all this punishment for nothing. To tell you the truth, he did feel a little pampered by his time at the river (No kidding!), and it was going to make the long long walk back home all that more arduous.

And it was. It was arduous and strenuous and taxing, and all those other synonyms. The heat, reflected by the desert sand and thrown back up into his face, was unbearable at times. Thirty-foot sand serpents burrowed in and out of the dunes all around him. Giant winged creatures swooped down out of the sky and ripped away at his flesh. It briefly occurred to him that maybe this was the punishment. But then he thought, no. No, the river was the punishment. (It also briefly occurred to him that he had very little concept of what punishment was.) At times he wanted to give up, but the thought of returning to Eve was enough to keep him trudging on.

At last, he arrived home. Eve was relaxing on the couch, her feet up on the ottoman. Her time must have been worse than his; she looked dead tired.

"Eve!" he exclaimed, and rushed to her side to embrace her. "You made it home!"

She nodded. Pa rum-pump-pum-pum. "I did. I'm glad to see you returned as well."

"Oh, sweetie," Adam said. "It was just terrible. Absolutely horrible. The water was wet and the hot sun kept making the drinks warm, and Phil Collins could be a right prick at times. Anyway, enough about me, how was your time in the Tigris? It must have been just horrendous."

"It was all right," she said.

"All right? Care to elaborate?"

"Not really," she said. She had already made her mind up. She wasn't going to tell him that she disobeyed him; it would not only make him angry, but it would surely destroy his ego. She would just let him cling to the idea that he was head of the house, and that she would do what he expected of her, if he thought it was for the greater good. She would think of it as her contribution to the wellbeing of the family.

"Fair enough," he answered. "Any word from God yet?"

"Nothing," said Eve. "Do you think we did the right thing, Adam? Do you think the punishment was enough?"

He sighed. "I don't know. I thought it was a good idea. But I assumed one of us would have heard from God right away. I was expecting visions while I was out there in the Jordan, but all I got was warm daiquiris. I have a feeling we're stuck here forever."

"Oh, I don't know," Eve said. She thought back to her chat with Satan, and how God wanted him to worship Adam. "I have a feeling you're in God's good graces."

"I sure hope so," said Adam. "Now, where's my boy?" he said at too high a volume.

"Shhh. I just put him down to sleep. He's been a hellraiser all day."

"So he survived his time alone, then?"

"Yes, he did just fine," she answered.

"Shit."

"Yeah."

A familiar face peeked around the corner. "Daddy!" Cain exclaimed, and ran to his father excitedly.

"There's my boy," he said, his arms wide open for a hug from his son.

The boy ran up to his father, punched him square in the nuts, giggled, and took off.

"Come back here you little shit!" he shouted. He turned to Eve. "Did you see that? That little... I'm gonna go teach him a lesson."

"No, don't honey. He's been waiting all day for you to come home so he could do that. Just let him go back to sleep so we can get some peace and quiet."

"You're right," he said. "Ugh, what do we do about him, Eve?"

"You know," she said, "I've been thinking. What do

you think about having another child?"

He couldn't shake his head fast enough. "Nuh-uh. No way. No no no."

"Listen. Just hear me out. Maybe this one would turn out to be a good one. We deserve a nice child, not one that goes around cauterizing the buttholes of little bunnies. Plus," she added, "I think it would do Cain a lot of good to have a playmate. Maybe he just acts out because he's bored. I mean, we're the only other people in his world, and who wants to hang out with adults all the time? Come on, what do you say? Let's have another baby."

And so, Abel was born unto the world. They called him Abel because they were hoping he would have a little more aptitude than his brother when he was born. Alas, it was not true. He was born a blubbering mass of tissue just like his brother. Although he was a lot more pleasant to be around, he was miles behind his brother in terms of overall brain capacity. He was a simple boy who'd never vivisect a desert rat like Cain, because he was gentle, yes, but also because he had no idea how to vivisect anything. In fact, he didn't know what vivisect meant. In fact, he had no understanding of words with more than two syllables.

16. Eve's Restless Night

And so time went on. The pipe dream that Eve had about Cain calming down and acting like a decent person once he had a brother was far-fetched. In fact, Cain became much worse. The special needs that Abel required demanded much of Adam and Eve's attention, plus, let's face it, they loved him more. So Cain was more than a little jealous.

Although Cain hated Abel with every ounce of his being, having his brother around did encourage his creativity, as he continually invented new ways to torture him. Covering him with honey and leaving him out in the desert sun to be eaten by fire ants, tying him up in the basement which he had to dig out himself just to have a place for his brother to tie him up in, removing him from his Friends and Family plan without notice. Cain was a cruel boy.

One night, Eve awoke startled from a most horrible dream. "Adam? Adam, wake up."

"Hmmm."

"Adam I have to tell you about the most horrible dream I had."

"Blrgr."

"Yes, yes. Later. But first you must listen while I tell you about my dream."

"Blrgr?"

"Oh, all right," Eve said, and performed her oral duties.

It wasn't clear to her why she did this, since it in no way gave her any pleasure. Also, it never yielded any children. Perhaps this was why Adam liked it so much. Maybe he was done with having kids. She couldn't really blame him after watching the shit-show that was Cain and Abel, day in and day out.

But what if it did produce a baby? A throat baby? She had never thought of that possibility, and there was good reason. The wisdom of the Fruit assured her that this was not biologically possible. So I'm not sure why I just brought that up.

Anyway, she finished, and spat in the chamber pot like usual. She should really clean that out someday. As he turned back around, she noticed a spot on his left inner thigh. A patch of dry skin, no more than a few centimeters across, resembling tree bark. She pulled it off without mercy.

"Yikes!" he shouted.

"Sorry," she said, and noticed that he was not bleeding. The light that the moon gave off coming through their cave window was enough to show that this fluid oozing out was not the dark, red fluid of normal blood. It had no color at all; it just glistened in the moonlight.

Maybe this is more of his manstuff, she thought, and lapped it up. No, it was not manstuff. It had a thicker, more sticky consistency, almost like glue, and had a faintly sweet taste to it. It reminded her of what the trees leaked on occasion.

"What was that?" Asked Eve.

"What was what?" he asked.

"That patch on your leg resembling tree bark."

"I don't know," he said. "I had the same thing on my shoulder the other day."

"I've never seen it before," she said, and he gave her a look. "What?" she asked.

"You have one too," he said.

"What? Where?"

He scraped a finger across her back in answer. She was petrified.

"What the... how did it get there?"

"I don't know," he answered. "You mean you hadn't noticed it?"

"No, I can't say I have. Well, don't just lie there, pull it off."

She read worry in his face. "What?" she asked.

"I um, don't think I can. It's taking up your entire back, almost."

"What?" she asked again.

"Yeah. It's huge."

"Where's it coming from?" she asked.

"No idea. Do you think it's an allergic reaction?"

"What does that mean?" asked Eve.

"I don't know. I thought you may know."

"Anyway, can I tell you about my dream now?"

"Absolutely, dear," Adam said, suddenly fully awake. She still had a couple minutes before the Sleep of Adam took over, so she had to make it quick.

"I dreamed that Cain was drinking Abel's blood."

"Okay," he said.

"What do you think it means?" she asked.

"I think it means that Cain is a lunatic. That's nothing new. Dream explained. Case closed. Anything else I can help you with?"

"I don't know. I'm worried about them, Adam. I think something bad is going to happen."

"Like what? Cain killing Abel? Let's be honest, honey.

Abel isn't the brightest bulb in the garden. If Cain kills him, it's survival of the fittest."

"Blasphemous Darwinist crap!"

"I'm just saying, is all."

Eve started to cry, and Adam put his arm under her and held her. "There, there," he said. "Look, if you're that worried about Abel, we'll keep them separated, okay? They can each have their own house far away from each other. That way nothing bad will happen."

"You promise?" she asked.

"Promise. I'll help build them both new huts tomorrow, first thing."

And so Eve, thus relieved of her anxiety, drifted back to sleep, not dreaming anymore about her two sons. Instead, she thought about the thing on her back just before she crossed over, and she dreamed a dream of becoming a giant tree.

She woke up, paralyzed, thinking she had turned into a tree in her sleep. Gradually, the feeling came back into her limbs, and she was able to speak.

"Adam?" she said.

"Blrgr," he answered.

"No, not again. I figured it out. I know what's causing the reactions with our skin. It's the Knowledge Fruits. Don't you see? This didn't happen until we started eating them. This is God's punishment for us."

"Ugh, Eve," he sleepily said, "God already punished us by banishing us to this awful place. That was it. The tree bark growing off of our skins and the twigs poking out from or pores is just a coincidence."

"Are you sure?" asked Eve.

"Positive. Now, go back to sleep."

17. A Talk with the Boys

The next day, Adam sat his two boys down on the couch.

"Ow! Quit it!" Abel shouted.

"Knock it off, Cain," Adam scolded.

"What is it, Dad? I'm awful busy," said Cain.

"Well, I've been doing some thinking. Seems you two boys can't get along. No matter how hard we try to get you to behave, it just keeps getting worse. I think it's time you both got jobs."

Groans from both of the boys.

"Aww."

"But Dad..."

"But Dad nothing. Your mother and I can't continue to live this way, listening to you fight all the time. Plus, we really need help around here. The crops are dying, and the animals are too. They all need tending to. Two people can only do so much. It's high time you chipped in."

"What do you want us to do, Dad?" Abel asked.

"Glad you asked. Abel, since you seem to have a way with animals, I'm going to train you how to be a shepherd."

"Cool."

"I thought you'd like that. As for you, Cain, I want you as far away from Abel as possible. You'll go down to the fields and be a husbandman."

"Haha!" Abel laughed. "Dad wants you to knock up the livestock."

Cain shook his head. "That's not a husbandman, you buffoon. A husbandman tills the soil. Which sounds like the complete opposite of something I want to do, Dad."

"Well, that's just a case of too bad, so sad, love Dad," Adam said. "We all have to do things we don't wanna do around here. Now, the ground is absolutely horrible, but I think we can grow better produce if the ground was tended to a little more. "

"Boring," said Cain.

"Now," said Adam, ignoring his son's comment, "let's get building you guys your own places to live."

"What?" both boys said at once, both for different reasons.

"Sweet!" said Cain. "I get my own pad!"

"Do I have to move out, Daddy?" Abel asked.

"You're both going miles away to do your jobs. It's not going to be an easy commute to go back and forth every day, especially since the wheel hasn't been invented yet. You'll have to stay at your respective farms, and only come back once a week with deliveries. Plus, we can't have you both living under the same roof. You'll kill each other."

Cain smirked, as though he had plans to do just that.

"Sounds like you want us to do all the work, Dad," Cain said. "What are you gonna do?"

"Never mind what I'm gonna do. I have a lot of stuff at home I have to take care of. I have to try to think of a way to get us back to Paradise, which means I have more penance to do. I have to take care of your mother. In a way you don't even want to know about. She wants sixty more children. Although I can't for the life of me even fathom the storm that will bring, she insists that it's the only way to save the human race. I've tried arguing that it's probably not worth saving, but she insists. I argued that that meant you boys would have to reproduce with your own sisters, and she explained that incest is not a sin, and there would be no complications as there are no mutant genes yet. I have a feeling she's been eating a lot more Forbidden Fruit than I have. Anyway, let's get you guys set up."

The boys walked in front of their dad. "Haha," Cain said. "You have to have sex with your own sister."

"At least I don't have to have sex with farm animals," Abel said.

"For the last time, that's not what a husbandman does!"

18. Trees

A couple weeks went by, and Cain killed Abel. I mean, let's face it, we all saw that coming. In fact, Adam was wondering what took him so long. Although he did wish it was the other way around, he wasn't overly upset about it. Eve, however, cried every day for the next nine months.

Until their next child Seth was born, which set off a cavalcade. Soon the children started pouring out of Eve like water out of a faucet. Sixty children they had in all. Not possible, you say? Impossible, others, who know their prefixes, say? Maybe for those with today's life spans. But when you take into account the fact that they lived for hundreds upon hundreds of years, it was a wonder all they had was sixty. They had stopped eating the Fruit of Knowledge, which not only stopped them from gaining any more intelligence, it also caused them to forget most of the stuff they had learned. One thing they did remember, which was perhaps the most important thing, was that the Fruit was turning them into trees. After years of not touching anything from the Trees, they noticed that no more twigs were growing out in random spots on their bodies, and their skin was taking back the normal consistency and glow of human skin, rather than bark.

"It sure is nice to not have to worry about turning into trees," Adam said.

Soon, however, despite their best efforts, the crops

began to die. All except one: the Knowledge Trees were in full bloom all the time.

"Well," Adam said, "we may be out of cucumbers and summer squash, but at least we have meat."

"Baaa!" He heard the sheep scream, and ran full tilt to the pens. One by one, they were dropping dead of massive coronaries.

"Hurry!" Adam shouted to Eve. "Grab some salt and some dry rub. We have to get these sheep butchered, dehydrated, and seasoned before the meat goes bad!" Immediately, the animal flesh started decaying right in front of their eyes and turned black, setting off a stink the likes of which they had never smelled. It was absolutely horrible, and made them both retch.

Adam turned to Phil Collins. "Sorry old buddy," he said. "You're going to have to make a sacrifice for the greater good."

Phil shook his head rapidly.

"Look at it this way, pal. You'll go down in history as a martyr. That's, like, the ultimate for a goat such as yourself, isn't it?"

"Gimme just one more night," Phil Collins said.

"Sorry, Phil. We love you, but you gotta go. Daddy's getting hungry."

The goat bolted, never to be seen again. In case you're curious, he went on to live a happy, healthy life. He found his way back to Eden, moved into luxury condo, met a lady goat, and started a family of his own. Generation after generation of talking goats later would spawn a most famous goat named Biddy, but that's a story for another time.

"Well, Eve. Looks like it's just you and me and a Knowledge Tree. What do we do now?"

"The only thing we can do," Eve said. "Let's dig in. I'm starving."

They both plucked a Fruit from the Tree.

"Let's do this together," Eve said. "On the count of three. Ready? One, two, three." And they both took a bite of their Fruits at the same time.

"You know," Adam said. "This is much better than I remembered."

"Yes," said Eve. "Much sweeter."

They both finished their Fruits and soon grabbed another. They plowed through those, and then on to the next. And the next, and the next. And much like salt water will only make you more thirsty, the Fruits made them more hungry. They found themselves gaining more knowledge than their human brains could handle. Some were things they had always wanted to know the answers to, and some things they felt they were better off not knowing. But they couldn't stop; they kept eating and eating. Their skin gradually turned to bark, and they paused every now and then to flick the random termite off of each other. After two days of constant eating, every Fruit on every Tree was gone.

"Now what?" asked Eve. "I'm still hungry."

"Me too, daddy," said Luluwa. The kids! He'd forgotten about the kids. After days of no food, they must have been starving.

"Oh, sweetie. You must be so hungry."

"Yes. We are about to start eating each other if we can't find something soon."

As if those words were a trigger, Fruits once again sprang forth from the Trees.

"Quickly," said Adam, "go forth and gather up your brothers and sisters and sons and daughters and nieces and nephews. Tell them there is plenty of Fruit to eat. We shall all become trees together."

"We shall all become what, daddy?" asked Luluwa.

"Oh, nothing. Hurry now, before your mother and I eat every last thing on the Trees."

A few hours later, and all the children were gathered around, noshing on the Fruits. Bark grew on Luluwa, and all their other children, and their children's children too. Roots grew from their toes, and sunk deep into the ground. Adam grabbed Eve's hand, and they were quickly frozen together.

"Daddy, what's happening?" Aklia asked, which set all the other children to asking their own questions, until their mouths became wooden and were unable to manage speech.

Adam tried to answer them, but alas, his mouth was frozen open as well.

A large forest stood where the children used to be.

The sky opened up, and the face of God appeared.

Why, God? Asked Adam in his mind. You owe me, no, you owe all of us, an explanation.

MYSTERIOUS WAYS? God responded.

That's not going to cut it. I have a feeling this was all a setup. Why did you do this? Why did you make Knowledge Fruit the only food available so that we all became trees?

CURIOUS WAYS? Said God, and if Adam could have given him a stern look, he would have.

OKAY, OKAY. YOU ALL BECAME KNOWLEDGE TREES SO THAT FUTURE GENERATIONS MAY EAT FROM YOUR BRANCHES, AND THEY MAY ALSO GATHER KNOWLEDGE, AND THEY TOO MAY BECOME TREES, SO THAT MORE GENERATIONS MAY DO

THE SAME. I HAVE BEEN DOING THIS FOR MILLENNIA.

Say what?

YOU REALLY THINK YOU AND EVE WERE THE FIRST ONES TO INHABIT THE EARTH? HA. THERE WERE SO MANY BEFORE YOU. ALL THOSE KNOWLEDGE TREES, THEY WERE ONCE PEOPLE. ISN'T THAT RIGHT, EUGENE? He asked a tree. HAHA, JUST KIDDING. I KNOW YOU CAN'T SPEAK. I LOVE PLAYING LITTLE GAMES LIKE THAT. KEEPS ME ENTERTAINED.

I still don't see the point, Adam said.

BECAUSE KNOWLEDGE IS A POWERFUL THING. BUT EVEN MORE POWERFUL IS WEALTH. DO YOU KNOW HOW MUCH MONEY KNOWLEDGE TREE WOOD IS WORTH UP HERE? AND YOU SHOULD SEE THE LOVELY FURNITURE THAT CAN BE MADE FROM THOSE LIKE YOURSELF. I'LL TELL YOU, YOU SHOULD BE PROUD TO BE A TREE.

Seems like a lengthy process to make a buck or two.

OH, God chuckled, I GOT TIME.

And so, dear reader, if you ever find yourself lost in the forest, and happen upon two old, wise looking trees that look like their branches are entwined, they just may be Adam and Eve, holding hands.

B is for

Bear

MARC RICHARD

1. That's Amore!

The lights beaming off the disco ball played tricks with the eye as they danced through Jimmy DiFreno's chest hair. He was quite proud of his chest hair. It was part of his culture to be proud of his chest hair.

He wasn't much to look at. He didn't have the classic chiseled looks of a Rudy Valentino or an Antonio Sabato Jr. One that could make the ladies swoon while simultaneously being a silent killer. No, he had the stereotypical looks of a James Gandolfini: Six-foot-two, two hundred seventy-five pounds, give or take. He knew that if he kept eating the way he did, he would most likely end up like the late great Gandolfini, but boy, did he love his *gabagool*. And spaghetti and meatballs. And *pasta fazool*. And pie. You get the picture. Not that he wasn't a good-looking guy in his own way; it's just hard to get people to believe that he wasn't in the mob with his appearance being the way it was. I mean, he was in the mob, in fact, he was the don; I'm just saying he couldn't hide the fact.

He usually dressed up very nicely in Armani suits, but when it came time to leave the cozy confines of his office in the back and get down on the dance floor of his own night club, Stella, he donned a pair of jeans and a button-down shirt, unbuttoned halfway, so that his marvelous chest hair could rustle like dried leaves in the wind. He also wore a gold chain, which further accented said chest hair, as well as said Italian heritage.

He was at Stella practically every day; however, he only came out on the floor a couple nights a week. The rest of the time was spent in the back room, doing books, or other types of lowdown, dirty business that was certainly not on the up and up. Stella was a front for a more lucrative, and less tax-collectible, business. Obviously. Every decent mafia crew had several legitimate businesses: laundromats, restaurants, night clubs, assassins-for-hire, birthday clowns, and on and on. A mob without a front to hide behind was like a freight train carrying a cargo of drugs and running over a beautiful Mexican woman who looked an awful lot like Salma Hayek. Not sure what that means? Jimmy did.

    He often got mistaken for a bear. No, not a real bear, since that would be weird to have a real bear in a club. Keep up, dummies. Since he was hairy, and large, and (some may even say) cuddly, occasionally he would be hit on by other men. He had an ironic vibe about him that most of the overly macho men of the bear persuasion were guilty of affecting. Like Freddie Mercury or Rob Halford, that kind of thing. It didn't happen too often, since this wasn't a gay club. But it happened often enough. And when it did, he would put on airs like he was offended. In reality, though, he was honored. Not that he'd ever have sex with them. He didn't swing that way. Except when it came to Joe.

    Most everyone in the mafia, and especially the dons, had a little *goomah* on the side. A don without a *goomah* was like a bald man picking up spare change. So that's why it came to Jimmy as a shock that his wife Charlene had no idea. Of course, there was a possibility that she did know and just chose to never bring it up, but he highly doubted it. You see, Charlene's father was Don Figarazzi, the don of the most famous Figarazzi family. The funny thing was, his name was also Don.

    Anyway, when he got to the age that he was "too old

for this crap", he handed the reigns to Jimmy. Sadly, he had no sons of his own, and since Charlene was the apple of Don's eye, it was his decision to give Jimmy the job. That way, his grandson could continue when he was old enough. Of course, this pissed off a lot of actual family members, including his brother Don, his nephew Donald, and his three cousins, Don, Don, and Timmy, but Don's decision was Don's decision, and so it stood.

Jimmy's father-in-law knew that he had a *goomah* on the side; it didn't really bother him. It wasn't his wrath he was concerned about. It was Charlene's. If she found out, not only would she cut his balls off, but she would also convince her father to have him taken out. Even though Jimmy was don, Don was still the don of the don, and there were plenty of actual Figarazzis that would have been more than happy to do the job.

Don Figarazzi would certainly have killed him if he knew just who Jimmy was fooling around on Charlene with. By now you probably have guessed that I am talking about Joe, since I mentioned it a while back. You see, homosexuality is frowned upon in the mafia community. It's a sign of weakness. In Italian dialect they call it a *fanook*, and Jimmy most definitely wasn't one. Now Joe, he wasn't so sure about, but really, who was he to cast aspersions? Joe was his capo, his best friend, and at times, his lover. That didn't necessarily make him gay, right?

Right?

You see, Joe saved Jimmy's ass in 'Nam. Joe nursed his dog to health when he didn't have a paw to stand on. Joe gave him a place to stay when he got out of the army and had no place to go. Joe rescued his mother from a burning building. He and Joe opened their first hot dog stand together, back when they were just kiddies in Brooklyn. Joe tipped him off on some winning lottery numbers. Joe gave him grape soda when he needed a fine carbonated beverage. All this you may already know; I'm not sure how much Jimmy has divulged to you. And tonight, he got himself a nice hummer in the bathroom. Not the truck, although he had one of those as well. And that would not fit in the bathroom. By hummer, I meant he got his dick sucked by Joe. Oh? I didn't have to explain that? You understood that already by the context? My bad.

Anyway, enough about Joe for now. The evening at Stella was at full swing, but Jimmy had his fair share of paperwork to do before he went home.

2. Meet the DiFrenzos

It was ten o'clock when Jimmy barged in. "Honey, I'm home!" he liked to shout, just like old Mr. Gleason used to do. And he was usually greeted with a warm embrace at the front door. However, Charlene was not in the mood for pleasantries. Despite the disheveled look she was sporting at the moment, she was still beautiful: tall, thin, long dark hair, gorgeous brown eyes he could swim in when he remembered to bring his trunks, and a usual look of adoration on her face. But not tonight.

"What's wrong, Charl?" he asked.

"Gimme the controller, jerk!" he heard his son call from the other room.

"That," Charlene answered.

"Who's he talking to?"

She sighed. "Your sister dropped her daughter off. It's been like this all day."

"What, the fightin'? Usually they get along."

"I think your niece is sick or something. She seems overtired, which has been setting Jimmy Junior off every five minutes."

"Don't worry," Jimmy said, and gave her a kiss on her forehead, "I'll straighten this out."

"Hey kids!" Charlene heard Senior say all friendly, like some big, dumb clown.

"Hey pop," Junior said.

"Hey Uncle Jim," his niece said.

Then the fighting continued.

"I said, gimme that!"

"Woah woah woah, the hell is goin' on?"

"She's been hogging the game," Junior said.

"So? She's your guest. And it's past ten. Get to bed."

"But daaaad..."

"But daaaad nothing. I'll be up to kiss you goodnight in a minute. Go on. Git."

He turned to his niece. "Your ma comin' to pick you up tonight?"

"Yeah, sometime," she answered.

"The whore," he muttered.

"What, Uncle Jim?"

"I said your mother is a lovely woman. Go on up to the guest room till your ma comes."

"Okay," she said, and headed upstairs.

He went back into the kitchen. "You all right?" he asked.

"Yeah, just tired. Kids."

"You sure nothing else is on your mind?" He got paranoid every time he had relations with Joe, and tonight, as I have already said, was one of those nights. Did she know something?

"No. Just the kids. Why?"

He kissed her on the forehead again. "No reason. I'm gonna go say goodnight to little Jim."

"Kiss him for me too," said Charlene. "I'd do it myself, but I've had more than enough for one evening."

"Sure thing."

He knocked gently on his son's bedroom door, even though it was cracked open like it always was. There he was, in his bed fast asleep. He must have been wiped.

Little Jimmy was eleven. Tonight was a bad example of the way the boy usually was. He was really a good kid. So well-behaved. And smart; he made the honor roll every quarter. He loved that little rugrat with all his soul, and hoped to God that he didn't follow in his old man's footsteps. Buuuutt, if he just so happened to follow in his old man's footsteps, Jimmy Sr. would be quite proud indeed. Just sayin'. He knew what the first signs would be. He would get a mouth on him. A lot of those in the family, they had kids with smart mouths, especially the boys. That's when it all would start, the downhill slide. They went straight from mouthing off to stealing candy from the corner store, right to gunning down rival families in the course of a year or two. Okay, so Jimmy was a little bit jealous. He shouldn't be; like I said, he was proud of Little Jimmy. But there was a part deep down that kinda wished he'd come home early from school for calling the teacher a twat-waffle or something.

The boy rolled over, and the light from the night-light lit his face up like a little cherub in a painting. His eyes were open.

"Dad?" he asked.

"Yeah?" he answered.

"I love you."

"I love you too, Jim. Very much." He brushed his son's hair out of his eyes and gave him a kiss on the cheek. "Good night, son."

"Good night."

Jimmy Senior turned to leave.

"Dad?"

"Yes?"

"I got somethin' to confess."

"I'm all ears."

"I got sent home from school today."

"What? Why?"

"I called the lunch lady a twat-waffle."

Lunch lady? Was that as good as a teacher? Yes, he was pretty sure it was.

"Shh. Go to sleep, son," he said, and left the room.

Charlene was sitting at the kitchen table.

"Honey, you look beat. Why don't you head on up to bed?"

"Yeah, I suppose I should. Wanna come up with me? Got time for some lovey lovey?"

"Not tonight, Charl. Too tired. I'm gonna do the dishes. Go on to bed, I'll be up in a bit."

She gave him a long kiss on his lips. "Night, honey. I love you. Thanks for doing the dishes."

"You're welcome. Love you too. Night, Charl."

And as he scrubbed the pots and pans, he couldn't help but smile, beaming.

"Lunch lady," he said. "How do ya like that?"

3. The Twat-Waffle Diaries

The following day was fairly uneventful. Jimmy spent most of the day in his office, balancing the books. If anyone had told him that the majority of being the boss would involve paperwork, he probably would have passed on the whole thing. In a way, he missed the action of being a capo, or even a soldier. Sure, the pay was nice, but whereas soldiers often suffered from gunshot wounds, he was suffering from boredom, which was ten times worse. He called a meeting just to keep from pulling his own hair out. It mostly consisted of things like *Why do you guys keep coming up light with the money*, and *We need to kill more people*, and things of that nature. You know, the typical. You've all seen the movies. Still, he'd much rather be in the office than have to go through what Charlene was doing at the moment.

She sat across the desk from the school principal. The look of disdain he gave her was something he would have been smacked in the mouth for, if her husband were here instead of her. That's why she was glad it was her there instead of him. Jim had a hard time keeping his cool when it came to people criticizing his son. By being angry at the principal, it would have been misdirected anger, she had to keep remembering that. Her ire should be aimed toward that little boy that was waiting in the hallway, the one that had called the lunch lady names.

"Listen, Mrs. DiFrenzo, Jimmy really is a good boy. He's one of the top students in his class, as you probably already know. If he just applied himself, and kept out of mischief, he could go really far in this world."

"Thank you," answered Charlene.

"But once in a while, he does things that we don't see in other children."

"Like calling the lunch lady a twat-waffle?" she asked.

"No, not at all. Had he called his teacher a twat-waffle, I would have suspended him instead of just sending him home. Miss Bean, the lunch lady, well, everyone calls her twat-waffle. You see, she has an unfortunate anatomical issue that, well, is unfortunate."

"I see."

"But that's neither here nor there," the principal said. "No, I'm afraid Jimmy's issues go much deeper than name calling."

"Like?"

"Like telling a boy he was going to have him whacked."

"He what, now?" she asked.

"He told a boy he was going to have him whacked. To be fair, Jimmy was just defending himself, as the boy has been known to be a bully. But when he used a word like *whacked*, well, given the circumstances with your family situation and all, the boy is now in fear of his life."

She glared at him, but he didn't notice.

"And the other day, we thought we'd bring back show and tell. I mean, nobody's too old for show and tell, right? Mrs. DiFrenzo, your boy brought a gun to school as his presentation. It was then we realized that maybe you *can* be too old for show and tell."

"He what?"

"He brought a gun to school. To be fair, it wasn't loaded, and he was only trying to teach the kids gun safety, but I don't think at his age he should have any authority to teach anyone about gun safety. And given the circumstances with your family situation and all, with his father being who he is, and your father being who he is..."

"What do you mean by *that*?" she just about shouted.

The principal's eyes widened as his life flashed before him. You had to choose your words properly when dealing with, well, you know.

"Uh, er, nothing. I'm sorry. Forget I said anything, okay? *Please?*"

She was beginning to think they should have enrolled him in a private Catholic school. The faculty there were used to dealing with mafiosi, and this wouldn't have been a big deal. In fact, they probably would have offered her some coffee when she went into the office. She wasn't offered any coffee here. Perhaps it was best they look into St. Mark's after all. Maybe her husband was right. Maybe public school wasn't the right fit for them.

"Yeah," answered Charlene. "All right. Water under the bridge." She got up to leave. "And thank you for your time, Bob," she said as she shook his hand. "My husband and I will be sure to have a long talk with Junior. I think there will be some major changes coming."

He grinned. Perhaps they would take him out of his school after all. That would certainly be a lot of weight off of his shoulders. "It was nice to see you again, Charlene," he said, as she headed toward the door.

"Please," she said, "call me Mrs. DiFrenzo."

And with that, she left his office and marched straight toward her boy waiting in the hallway.

"How did it go in there?" he asked.

"You brought a *gun* to school? *Seriously*?"

"It's never too early to learn about gun safety, mom."

"You can't bring a gun to school. These days, with all the school shootings? What the hell is wrong with you?"

"I guess I..."

"And telling a boy you were going to have a hit taken out on him?"

"I hate it here, mom. I hate *everyone* here. And I think my exact phrasing was that I would have him whacked."

"You can't say that!" she yelled. "Especially given the circumstances with our family situation and all."

"Just what is our situation, mom?"

"Never mind," she said. "There is no situation."

"When am I finally going to learn the truth about what dad does, and what grandpa did?"

"Your dad owns a club. That's it. It's no secret."

"Yeah, but that's not all he does, is it?"

She sighed, and looked at her watch. It was still early.

"Come on," she said, "let's go get some breakfast. I'll call your dad and he can meet us at IHOP and we can talk about alternative schooling options. Whaddaya say?"

"Yes! I'm starving," he answered. "I could sure go for some waffles."

4. Blondie

Her name was Marguerite but everyone called her Blondie. A spoiled little rich bitch. That was how others described her, and to her that seemed pretty fair. She *was* a spoiled little rich bitch. There wasn't a moment in her seventeen years of life where she wanted for anything. Everything she had ever asked for, she got. And then some. Her father was killed years ago, and her mother tried getting her though the grieving process not by love and understanding, but opting for the easier way of parenting: showering her with monetary affection.

She was a beautiful girl with big blue eyes, long blond hair, and a figure to die for. For a teenager she was quite well-developed. I am not going to go into specifics, lest I be considered a pervert, but let's just leave it at she was very attractive. She could have any boy she wanted, but she didn't want boys. Or girls, for that matter. No, what *really* turned her on was danger.

Years ago, the tedium of spoiled rich bitch life had gotten to her, and that's when she started breaking into homes. She had never taken anything from anyone, since she already had everything she wanted. The excitement was in the unlawful entry. It was just something fun to do, to see if she could get away with it. She was pretty good at it, too, only getting caught one time out of the hundred or so houses she broke into. The owners had caught her sleeping in their bed, and were about to call the police when she prattled on with her well-rehearsed story about her being a homeless orphan with no place to go. They felt sorry for her, fed her some porridge, and offered to adopt her. The only caveat, they told her, was that once in a while she would be called upon to do favors for her new adopted father of the intimate variety, since his wife was a quite frigid woman. By the time the mother-to-be explained the wonders of Hershey's chocolate syrup, she had bolted out the front door, never to be seen again. Weirdos.

This little incident didn't stop her from breaking into homes, however. Quite the contrary, in fact. It added a little more excitement to the whole deal. I mean, she knew deep down there was always a possibility of getting caught, but now that it had actually happened, it made it that much more real. And now, here she was, standing in back of a house that belonged to the biggest mob family in the city. This was it. The pinnacle of her breaking and entering days had finally come.

The DiFrenzos' home was fully equipped with a state-of-the-art security system and the best locking mechanisms for doors and windows money could buy. There was no sense in skimping. Being who he was, Jimmy had spared no expense in keeping his family safe. Nothing in the world was more important than the well-being of his wife and kid.

She got past all that by throwing a rock through a rear window. This set the alarm off, but by this point, she was quite the professional. Within seconds, it was disarmed.

Wow, this was the life. *Just look at this place,* she thought. Sure, her family had money, but nothing at all like this. So this is what blood money bought you. The biggest house on the block, with all the nicest things. Everything was so state-of-the-art, so excessive. She loved it. However, right now she had something in her eye.

She found her way to the bathroom. One of many, she was certain. Rich people always felt the need to have more bathrooms in their homes than they had people living there. Her own family was no exception with five. She wasn't quite sure why this was the case. It was just more to clean. Although, let's be real, her family didn't clean anything. That's what they had the Guatemalan maid for. Sure, they could have used a service like Happy Maids, but to have a true Guatemalan, that really screamed something about their status.

She looked in the mirror and examined her eye. An eyelash had gotten in it. This happened frequently, as she had such long, gorgeous eyelashes. She gave her eyeball a swipe with the tip of her finger and removed the offensive lash.

Sweet. Now her eye was irritated. She looked in the medicine cabinet for some Clear Eyes or something. Nothing there to help her eye, but there were some Oxycontins that she decided to pocket for later.

She had never in her life seen a triple vanity, but the DiFrenzos had one, each with their own sets of drawers. All stenciled with their names: Jim Sr., Charlene, Jim Jr. Wasn't that just darling? She opened the drawer that belonged to Jim Jr. Nothing in it but a Spongebob toy and a bottle of hair gel, medium crispy. In Charlene's drawers she found the typical woman stuff: emergency makeup, curling iron, straightening iron, and hair gel, low crisp. Jim Senior's drawers held nothing but seventy-two types of aftershave and a bottle of hair gel, EXXXTreme Crisp. She tossed all three bottles of hair gel on the floor in a brief moment of frustration. Nothing for her eye. Oh well, the irritation should go away in a little bit; it was time to explore some more.

Suddenly hungry, she went to the kitchen to see if they had anything good to eat. What a massive kitchen it was! And so fancy. Marble counter tops, marble floors, a Viking stove, Sub-Zero refrigerator, all the best equipment. And so clean! There wasn't a cutting board in the sink, no signs of spillage on the stove. She would bet money on them getting takeout all the time. Generally when someone had a kitchen this nice, they rarely used it. Perhaps there was something in the fridge anyway.

Not much, apparently. Beer, white wine, lots of condiments, some sandwich meat. Three kinds of capicola! She opened the plastic bag with the first variety in it. Spicy capicola. She'd never had the spicy kind. Wooh! Too hot. She threw the bag of meat across the room. In the second bag was sweet capicola. Almost too sweet, though. It tasted like it was honey cured and then they poured more honey on it when they were done curing it. Too much. She threw that one across the room as well. She opened the third bag to taste that one. That was just right. The proper blend of spice and sweet. Finding some bread in the box on the counter, she decided to fix a sandwich.

Wonder what's on tv? Blondie asked herself. She flopped down on the beanbag chair in the corner like she was a three hundred pound octopus. A slight tear in the bag allowed the beans to spew out all across the room. This chair was too soft. She tried the recliner. Most likely that belonged to Jimmy DiFrenzo himself; most men of his ilk had their own special chairs that no one else was allowed to sit in. It looked quite comfortable, but sitting in it was a different story. Too hard. It had that feel that some furniture gets before you break it in. Since she figured Jimmy had spent a lot of time in front of the tube, and his massive frame would break in a chair in no time, it must have been new. She was more of a couch girl, anyway, and she sauntered on over to the sofa and got herself comfy. It felt just right. It was so comfortable, in fact, that for the first time in her life, she considered stealing something. Her couch at home was too formal; okay to sit in, but not cushy enough to lie down on. Unfortunately, her mother just *loved* the couch, and all their guests just *loved* the couch, and there was no way she could swap it out and have people not notice. Also, she couldn't move a couch by herself. No, this was a couch dream, and couch dreams were for sissies and baseball players, for Christmas carol crooners and turkey stuffers.

She turned on the tv and was instantly irritated. No Roku, no Amazon Fire Stick, just straight cable. She'd heard of cable tv before, but had never witnessed it. Such an antique concept. It should have been charming that these people were holding onto old tradition, but it was annoying as hell to her. She flipped through the channels, discouraged that she had to deal with what was on right at that moment instead of being able to pick any show she wanted. How disturbing. It didn't make sense. They were rich. Why in the world would they... oh well. It didn't matter. She checked her cell phone for the time. Ten o'clock. The DiFrenzos wouldn't be home for a while yet, not until Junior got out of school, anyway.

She flipped through the channels till she stumbled upon *The People's Court*. Seemed pretty interesting. She took a bite of her sandwich. The combination of Wonder Bread and mayonnaise stuck to the roof of her mouth. She needed something to wash it down with. *May as well help myself to a beer or three,* she thought. Although she liked to consider herself a rebel, she really wasn't much of a drinker, and by the time she'd finished her third beer, she was fast asleep on the couch.

5. Who's the Bimbo?

After a nice breakfast at IHOP, the DiFrenzos all headed home, Charlene and Junior in her Hummer, and Jimmy in his. Charlene got herself and Junior out of her vehicle, and was headed for the front door when Jimmy came out of his own vehicle, and yelled, "Wait!"

She turned to her husband, and he shook his head. "Somethin's not right here," he said.

"What's not right here?"

"Look. Right through the livin' room window. Notice somethin'?"

"What am I noticing?" she asked.

"You don't see it? You left the fuckin' tv on again. How many times, Charl? How many times have I had to tell you that electricity costs money and money don't grow on bushes and whatnot?"

"Three hundred," she said. "But it wasn't me."

"Junior, how many times have I told you that money don't grow on bushes and whatnot?"

"Five hundred," he said. "But it wasn't me."

"Well," said Jimmy, "if it weren't you, and it weren't you, then who was it? Did someone break into our unbreakable house and turn the tv on?"

"That's crazy," Charlene said.

"Preposterous," Junior echoed with a different word. He had obviously been spending a lot of time with his new thesaurus.

"Ludicrous," said Jimmy, who had also glanced occasionally at the thesaurus.

"There's no need to bring his name into this," said Charlene, who was feeling bad that she'd only used a word with two syllables.

"Hmm," said Jimmy. "Must be a ghost or somethin'. Come on, let's go in, I'm hungry."

"Hungry?" Charlene asked. "You just ate a huge breakfast."

"Yeah, but you know what they say about pancakes. Eat as much as you want, in an hour or so you'll be hungry again."

Charlene never heard this expression. Pancakes always made her feel like she ate more of them than she actually did.

Jimmy shouted from the kitchen. "Hey, you wanna sandwich?"

"Are you kidding me right now?" Charlene said.

"Junior?" he asked.

"I'll have a dry martini."

"Wiseass," Jimmy replied. He rifled around in the refrigerator for a second, then said, "Hey! What happened to all the *gabagool*?"

"What are you talking about?" she said from the entryway. "We had three bags of it."

"Yeah, well, not no more. Somebody's been eating my *gabagool*."

Charlene stepped into the kitchen. "Who would eat your *gabagool*? It's too spicy."

"I don't know, but somebody did. There's a couple slices missin'."

"What are you, counting slices now?"

"I know when food is missin', believe me."

"Well, you're the only one who eats that hot stuff. My sweet *gabagool* is right here in this...hey! Somebody's been eating my *gabagool*!"

"What are you, countin' slices?" he echoed.

"Yes," she answered.

Just then, Junior ran into the kitchen to see what all the fuss was about.

"What's wrong?" he asked.

"Somebody's been eating *my gabagool*," said Dad.

"Somebody's been eating *my gabagool*," said Mom.

Junior looked in the fridge, then on the counter, where his empty bag lay.

"Somebody's been eating my *gabagool*," he said. "And they ate it all up!"

"I don't like what's goin' on here," said Jim Senior.

"Hold that thought," Charlene said. "I gotta pee."

A few seconds went by, and then, "Ahhhhh!"

Dad and Junior rushed into the bathroom. "What is it?" Dad asked.

"Somebody's been messing with my hair gel!" she yelled.

"What the?" said Dad. "Somebody's been messing with *my* hair gel."

"Somebody's been messing with *my* hair gel," said Junior, "and spilled it all over the place."

"I don't like what's goin' on here," repeated Jim Senior. "I got a baaaad feelin'."

"Go check the rest of the house," Charlene told Jim.

"Wait here," he said to his wife and son, and went into the living room.

"Woah woah woah," he said. "Somebody's been sittin' in my chair."

"What are you talking about?" asked Charlene. "Nobody in their right mind would, oh no. Look at that. It's all reclined. And what the hell happened to Jimmy's bean bag chair?"

"What about my bean bag chair?" Junior asked as he entered the room, and instantly he started to cry. "Somebody broke my bean bag chair!" he wailed.

"I don't like what's goin' on here," said Jim Senior for the third time.

A smack landed across his face. "Hey!" he said. "What's your problem, Charl?"

"Somebody is laying on my couch," she said. "Who's the bimbo?" She pointed to the blond girl, still passed out.

"How the hell should I know?" he said in defense.

"Caught you red-handed," she said.

"Yeah," said Jim. "Caught you red...hey, wait. You talkin' to me?"

"Yes, I'm talking to you. I told you if I ever caught you with a *goomah*, we were through. And now, here she is, in our own house? And she can't be more than sixteen. Disgusting."

"You fuckin' kidding me right now?" he asked. "Junior, cover your ears. You think I'm fuckin' around with *this*?" He gestured at the sleeping girl.

"Oh, come on," Charlene said. "I know all about you men and what you get up to. My family was torn apart because of my dad's mistress. Don't give me that shit. You're all the same."

He cradled Charlene's face in his hands, slightly forceful, but not enough to hurt. "Charl, I ain't like the other guys. I ain't sleepin' with no *woman* behind your back. And if I was, do you think I'd invite him here, of all places?"

"Invite him here?" she echoed.

"Invite who here?" he asked.

"You just said invite him here," she said.

"Not sure who you're talkin' about. Invite who here? You know nobody's invited here unless they're invited."

"Then who is this?" she asked.

"That's just what I intend to find out. Junior, go to your room."

"But dad..."

"Don't but dad nothin'. Go to your room. Now."

He sighed and stomped up the stairs, slamming his door.

Jim took a seat on the couch beside the girl.

"Hey. Hey Blondie, wake up."

She stirred, but not enough to awaken.

Jim hit her open-handed across the face.

"Ow! What the..."

"Jim, there's no need of that," Charlene said.

Ignoring his wife, he said, "Good mornin', sleepy head."

"Wha...? Where am I?"

"You're in the wrong fuckin' house, that's where you are." He breathed heavily through his nose, steam coming out of his nostrils. Her dazed look turned to one of fear. It was obvious she hadn't expected to have fallen asleep, and it was certainly obvious she hadn't expected to get caught.

"Wrong house!" she said. "That's it! Oh, man. Sorry, I thought this was my house. They look identical, you know. Except you don't live in my house, so this must not be my house. Yes, that's it. Common mistake. Well, I'm sorry to disturb you lovely folks. I'll just be on my way. Can you point me the way to Cavendish?"

"Wrong house, huh?" Jim said. "Well, of course.

Happens all the time." He smiled. "Cavendish is about three miles that way." He pointed his finger.

"Ah, well thank you very much. Sorry for the inconvenience."

His smile became more sinister. "No problem, really. I guess you'll be on your way, then?"

"Yes. Let me just grab my...Where are my shoes? I know I put them somewhere."

He pointed by the door.

"Ah, yes well, again, sorry for all the trouble. Won't happen again, I promise."

As she opened the door to leave, two police cruisers quickly pulled into Jimmy's driveway. Officer Roberts got out of his vehicle and shot Jimmy a friendly wave. He responded with the same gesture.

She turned to him, angrily. "You called the cops on me? What the fuck? Why would you do that? I told you it was a mistake."

"Oh really?" he said. "Do you make it a habit of breakin' your own window?" he gestured to the broken glass.

"What seems to be the trouble, Jimmy?" officer Roberts asked.

"Seems we have ourselves a little intruder," he answered.

"Is that right?" Roberts asked.

"Little bitch broke my window and ate my *gabagool*."

"She ate your *gabagool*?"

"Yep. You know the rule: Never touch another man's meat." The irony was not lost on him.

"Are you the person who's been breaking into homes all throughout the tri-county area?"

"I thought they were mine," she responded.

"Come with me, missy. We're going downtown."

She glared at Jimmy. "I can't believe you called the cops."

"Believe me, honey," he said, "it beats the alternative."

Roberts laughed. "Sure does," he said, "It sure does."

He waved a childish wave to the blond girl as she got in the back of the cruiser. "Bye-bye!" he shouted. "Don't be a stranger!"

She shot a finger out the rear window at him. A very bold move indeed, but at this point she had very little to lose.

6. Porridge

Blondie had been lucky most of her life. This was her first run-in with the law, and definitely her first time in jail. She hadn't even had any idea what the inside of one looked like until now. She needed to get out of here as quickly as possible, maybe even quicker than that.

Officer Roberts came around with a tray of food. "How ya doin', rich girl? Not used to this, are ya? I brought you some food."

He set the tray on the floor and slid it underneath the bars of her cell.

The officer looked at the steaming bowl of slop, and then at her, in much anticipation. Like he expected her to eat this.

"What is this?" she asked.

"Cream of Wheat," he answered.

"You mean *porridge*?"

"I guess so. Not a fan, huh?"

"Not really. Reminds me of a time I'd rather not think about."

"Well, you need to get used to it if you're going to live a life of crime. Your diet will consist of nothing but porridge and bologna sandwiches. And every Wednesday is lobster mac n' cheese."

"Fancy," she said.

"Not really," he said, guiltily. "It comes in frozen."

"Well, I'm not going to have time to get used to it. I'm getting out of here as soon as they set bail."

"Good for you," he said. "You know, today could have turned out a lot worse for you. I've seen some of the things that happen to people who end up on the bad side of Jimmy DiFrenzo, and it ain't pretty, let me tell you. Why, I could tell you tales that would make your skin crawl."

"Ooh, do tell," she said.

"You know, I really shouldn't. He's never been convicted of a crime, so I probably should just leave it alone. But, since you asked so nicely, I guess it wouldn't hurt to tell you a few things. Remember that movie *8 Heads in a Duffel Bag*?"

"Yeah."

"Well, how about nine heads in a duffel bag?"

"So?"

"So? It was one more head than the movie. Scary, huh?"

"That's nothing."

"Remember the movie *A Series of Unfortunate Events*?"

"Yeah."

"Well I knew a guy that after he double-crossed ole Jimmy, he was met with a series of even worse unfortunate events."

"And...?"

"And what?"

"What were they?"

"They were even worse unfortunate events. You know, like, *really bad*."

Blondie yawned.

"Okay, okay, here's one. You know that movie *Pulp Fiction*?"

"Yeah, yeah?" she said excitedly.

"Well sometimes people who double-cross Jimmy are left in a bloody pulp. And they *wished* it was fiction."

"All you're doing is taking movie titles and twisting them up all silly. Can you give me some real dirt on the guy?"

"Okay, last one. You know the movie *Fargo*, right?"

"Yes, I know the movie *Fargo*."

"Well, one time someone double-crossed Jimmy, they had to move to Fargo to hide from him."

"And? Did he find the guy and separate his body parts? Did he toss him over a bridge with cement shoes? Did he give him to a guy in a Skyhawk who tossed his body into the frigid Arctic Ocean, where he soon froze into a block of ice?"

"Nope. Never found the guy."

"Has anyone ever told you that your stories are like, really boring?"

"Whatever. Eat your porridge. It ain't getting any tastier just sitting there."

She didn't have to spend the night there; however, she must have been dead tired, because before she knew it, she was sound asleep. She awoke in the morning refreshed. That night she spent in the cell was the best sleep she'd had in a long time. Anyway, it was time to go pay bail and get the hell out of there.

Officer Roberts opened the cell door.

"Where do I go to pay?" she asked.

"Right up at the window in the lobby," he said.

"Cool. Hey, thanks for all the laughs."

"Keep it moving." He gave her a fatherly look. "And I don't wanna see you back here, understand?"

"Whatever, after-school special. It's been real."

She got up to the window.

"Can I help you?" the old gentleman behind the glass asked. He must have been a hundred and six years old if he was a day.

"Yeah, I'm here to pay my bail."

"Name?"

"Marguerite Bonaventure."

"Bonaventure...Bonaventure... let's see." He put on his reading glasses and perused through the list.

"Let me see," he repeated.

"Come on, pops. There ain't nobody else here. The list can't be too long."

"Let's see, Bradley, nope, Bauer, nope. Bonneville, hey you sure it's not Bonneville?"

"What's the bail for Bonneville?"

"Ten thousand."

"Nope. Bonaventure. You know, as in not Bonneville."

"Ah. Here it is. Bonaventure. First name?"

"How many Bonaventures are listed? I just told you. Marguerite."

"Ah yes, Marguerite Bonaventure. Let's see. Um. Let's see here. Oh yes, here it is, Marguerite Bonaventure."

"Jesus Christ, can you speed it up a little?"

"Ah yes, Marguerite Bonaventure. Let me see here. Oh, um... yes, that's it. That'll be forty-eight dollars and uh, let's see... sixty-three cents.

"Okay, well you have my purse, so..."

"Your purse?"

"Yeah, you know, the thing ladies carry around to keep their money in?"

"Ah yes, your purse. Hmm, okay. Purses, now lemme see, where do we keep the purses?"

"You're kidding me."

"Ah, here they are. Now, what does your purse look like?"

"It's Vera Bradley."

"I thought you said you weren't Bradley. You said you was Bonaventure."

"No, the purse is... never mind. Just show me what you have, and I'll pick it out."

"Well, we only have the one here. Is this it?" he pulled her purse off the holding shelf.

"Yeah, that's it," she said in a get-me-the-hell-out-of-here tone. "If that was the only one, why... ah, forget it. Just hand it over."

"Okay, here ya go, sweetie."

She opened her wallet and pulled out her credit card. "Here."

"Oh, no. We only take cash here."

"You gotta be shitting me," she said.

"Sorry. That's the law. No credit cards for bail."

"Well. Here, then." She handed him two twenties and a ten. Good thing she kept cash on her at all times.

"Fifty dollars? I'm afraid I don't have change."

"You don't have change? You're a cashier, for Godsake."

"They don't give me change."

"Why such a strange amount set for bail, if you don't have change?"

"It's set by an algorithm I can't fathom," he answered.

"Fine, then. Keep the change."

"Oh, no, I can't do that. Exact change only. That's the law."

"Nowadays it's pure luck anyone would have cash on them at all, never mind exact change. Come on, can't you let me slide this once?"

"Afraid not," the old guy answered.

"There's nothing I can do to get out of here today?"

"Call your folks," he said.

"Can't do that. My mom doesn't know anything about this."

"Call a friend."

"Don't have those."

"Call an aunt or uncle."

"They'd just tell my mom."

"Show me your boobies."

"I don't think that... wait, what?"

"Show me your boobies and I'll forget you don't have exact change." A line of drool exited his gaping maw and dropped onto the floor with a sickening *thud*.

"Fine," she said, and raised up her shirt for him as though she'd done it for hundreds of old men in her lifetime. She had, actually, but that's a story in itself.

The old man's wig flipped off his skull, and his glass eye popped out and rolled onto the counter and onto the floor, where it ended up swimming in his saliva pool, calling for help.

"Hot diggity dog!" he shouted, and hit the button that unlocked the door that would release her back into the wild.

It sure was nice to feel the sunshine on her face again. Now, to get her revenge on DiFrenzo.

7. It's Good for Stains, Though.

"What do you got for me, Lou?"

Lou hands over the envelope. Jimmy feels it in his hand for a brief moment.

"Little light," he says.

"Yeah, I know. I'll get you next week."

"Lou, you been sayin' that every week. When you gonna come through?"

"Next week, I swear."

Jimmy nods. Lou knows that nod. "I was being generous. It's a lot light."

There were eight people in the room, but there was the sound of zero. You could hear the proverbial pin drop.

"Look, I know this job ain't for everyone. And if you can't hack it, then maybe you need to find a different line of work."

"Look, Jimmy, I..."

"Don't I treat you good?"

"Sure?"

"Benefits not good enough for you? Health insurance and the like?"

"No, the benefits are fine, Jimmy, I..."

"Need another week's vacation?"

Lou knew that sometimes "vacation" didn't mean *vacation*. They all knew that. Everyone in the room was silently praying to the Blessed Virgin that Lou would make it till next week. All except Bobby. He had bet against Lou making it another week, and he had a lot of money riding on it.

"Yeah, boss. Maybe he needs another vacation," Bobby said, getting the look of death from Lou.

"Yeah," said Jimmy. "Maybe he does after all."

Lou gulped a loud, cartoonish gulp that was heard not just by those in the room, but by everyone out in the bar and on the dance floor of Stella.

Jimmy reached into the inside pocket of his sport coat as Lou braced himself for the inevitable. He slowly pulled his hand out from his pocket, revealing an envelope of his own. "Here," he said, handing the envelope to Lou.

"What's this?" Lou asked.

"Two tickets to Cancun. Take Victoria and get away for a while. I was gonna take Charl, but you obviously need it more than I do."

"Gee, I don't know what to say. Thanks, boss."

"Forget about it. Go. Get away. Clear your head. When you come back, I need you back in the game a hundred percent. *Capisce*?"

"Sure thing, Jimmy. You can count on me."

"Good. Now get outta here, you rapscallion."

"You bet! I'll pack tonight!"

"Now, Bobby. You had a lot to say earlier. Where's your envelope?"

"Here it is, boss," he said, and handed his own envelope over.

Jimmy weighed this one in his hand. "Hmm. It's a *lot* light."

"It's all there, boss. Count it."

"Don't tell me what to do!" he shouted. "Think I'll count it." He opened the envelope and dumped out the contents. Inside were a dozen handwritten checks.

"The fuck is this? Checks?"

"Yeah."

"Since when do we take checks, boss?" asked Joe

"I got this, Joe," said Jimmy. "Since when do we take checks, Bobby?"

"Well, see, I was thinkin',"

"Oh, this oughtta be a good one. Yeah? You were thinkin'?"

"Yeah, see, walkin' around with big wads of cash? Very dangerous. I could get robbed and whatnot. So I axed my customers to pay me by check. See, that way, I don't get robbed or nothin'."

Jimmy finished counting the amounts on the checks. "All here," he said.

"See? I told ya. I wasn't gonna stiff you or nothin'. Now, where's my vacation?"

"Oh, yours is coming. Joe, take this guy for a walk. Explain to him about checks and whatnot."

Joe led Bobby out of the room and up the elevator ten stories, the top floor of the building. As they walked down the corridor and toward the door that went to the roof, Joe talked about the magic of checks.

"See, Bobby, every week you come in here light, right?"

"Yeah, I guess I do," he said, embarrassed.

"It's not a big deal. People come in light all the time. It happens. We can let these accounts float for a week or so. Business has its ups and downs week to week; we get that. They just pay us a little extra the following week. It's how it's done. We make more money in the long run that way. Now, here you come with a handful of checks. Every cent paid. See the issue?"

"Nah. I don't see no issue."

"See, there's a reason we're a cash only business. Why do you think that is?"

"I don't know. Personally, I think we're doing it wrong."

"Okay, there are two problems with checks as I see it. One, is they're traceable. Now, if you had half a brain in your head, you would get why that isn't a good thing. Not least of which is taxes, and also the certain legalities or lack thereof of the business we're in."

He put his arm around Bobby's shoulder, leading him to the edge of the roof. Bobby was sweating profusely.

"You know another thing about checks, Bob?"

Tears sprang from Bobby's eyes as he shook his head vigorously.

"Come on, Bobby. Dry your eyes. Have some respect. I asked you a question. Do you know another thing about checks?"

"N-n-no," Bobby stammered.

"They bounce," Joe said, as he pushed him off the edge.

Joe strolled back into the office, whistling a tune.

"Ay! How'd you make out? He understand our check policy now?"

"Oh yes. He won't be making that mistake no more."

Dollars flew in all directions, as those betting that Bobby wouldn't last through the week won their bets.

"You know, it really ain't appropriate, you guys makin' money off betting on the way I run my practice. What's this?" he asked, pointing to the pile of money in front of him.

"You won the bet too, Jimmy," Joe said.

"Ha! Well I'll be. Who wants some drinks? On me."

All raised their hands.

"Shirley Temple for you, Wagon Boy?" Jimmy asked Michael Imperioli, who was two years clean and sober.

"Yeah, the usual."

"You know, I'm awful proud of you, Wagon Boy," Jimmy said. "But if you're not gonna drink, at least order something a little more manly, like a club soda."

"But club soda's fucking disgusting," Michael Imperioli said.

And he was right; club soda was fucking disgusting.

"Yo, Tammy. The usual round for the usual dummies. 'Cept you can hold off on Bobby's drink. I don't think he'll be needing it."

Tammy stopped wiping a glass with her bar rag and chuckled. "Is that him I just heard hit the pavement out there?"

"Yeah. Dunno what happened. One minute he went out on the roof for a smoke, and the next... I told him smokin' was gonna kill him one day. Remind me tomorrow to have someone put guardrails up there. This can't happen again."

Tammy laughed again. "Sure thing, Jimmy."

"How you doin' honey?" Jimmy asked the girl sitting at the bar nursing a drink of her own. "You okay?"

"Yep. Just finishing up here." The girl slammed down the rest of her beverage and got up off her stool. She turned to face him. "You know, you have a really nice establishment."

He recognized that face. "Blondie?"

She put on her coat and walked toward the door with a friendly wave. "Think I just found my new watering hole," she shouted to a flabbergasted Jimmy as she went out.

8. Your Ma Made Lasagna

"Hey Charl," he said when he strolled through the door. She gave him a kiss, and he kissed her back with much gusto.

"Mmm. Tough day at the office?" she asked.

"How'd you know?"

"You always kiss me like that when you've had a rough day."

"I do? Ha. I never noticed. I needed to feel your lips against mine for a while."

"Awww."

All that was wrong with the world just melted away every time he kissed her. She was his everything. It was a shame he slept around on her with Joe, but Joe had one thing she didn't have. A tattoo. Ha. Just kidding. Of course I meant cock.

"Where's our child?" he asked.

"He's in his room."

"What's he doin' there?"

"No idea. Now that I think about it, I haven't seen him all day. I was wondering why it was so peaceful here."

Knock knock.

"Come in."

Jimmy opened the door to find Junior lying in bed, reading a book. So studious!

"Hey, Champ."

"Hi Dad."

"Whatcha doin' in here?"

"You told me to go here."

"I did?"

"Remember? When the girl was here?"

"That was yesterday," said Jimmy. "You haven't come out since?"

"Nobody told me I could."

"For the life of me, I don't understand how you get straight A's."

"*Used* to get straight A's. I don't know how I'm gonna do at St. Mark's."

"You'll do fine, kid. Your dad went to St. Mark's, and look how he turned out."

A tear came to Junior's eye.

"Hey, now. I find that kind of insultin'."

"Sorry, Dad. Nothing against you. I just, I don't know. I guess I'm excited to go, but a little nervous too. What if I don't make any friends?"

"You didn't have friends at your old school," answered Jimmy.

A few more tears rolled down Junior's cheeks.

"Aw, come on. I didn't mean that. Listen, you know half the kids going there. You'll be fine."

"You really think so?"

"I do," said Jimmy, as he picked at his teeth with his heavily ringed pinky finger.

"Something in your teeth?"

"Yeah. Think it's *gabagool* from yesterday."

Junior broke into a full-on sob

"Now what's the matter?" his dad said.

"Somebody ate all my *gabagool*."

"You can have some of mine."

"It's too spicy!" he wailed.

"For the love of... Come eat. Your ma made lasagna. You must be starvin'."

"I haven't eaten anything all day," said Junior.

"Why not?"

"Nobody told me I could."

"Hold on a second," Jimmy said, and pulled out the back of his boy's pants..

"What are you doing?"

"Makin' sure you're wipin' your ass. Nobody told you to do that either."

They went down the stairs together.

"Dad?"

"Yeah?"

"Do you *really* think I'll like St. Mark's?"

"I do. I really do. Now, let's eat," he said, then mumbled, "Your dad wants to go to the titty bar."

"What's *that*?" Junior asked.

"I said your ma's lasagna is the best by far."

"Sure is," Junior said.

9. The Blue Iguana

The Blue Iguana wasn't the best strip club in the city, and it wasn't the worst. It was a very medium-type place. It had re-opened just a little over a year ago, after the place was burned to the ground by a Molotov cocktail a disgruntled employee threw through a window. The tits were good, and on nights like tonight they were just plain weird, but the food was pretty damn fantastic for pub food. And it was never really busy like the places further downtown, so Jimmy could go and relax and get his mind off of things. Tonight was a typical night at the club, except it was the first Friday of the month. First Fridays were called "Freaky Fridays" at the Iguana, and they were anything but typical, so this, being a first Friday, was also a Freaky Friday, and it wasn't really typical at all.

"...And next on the stage, the tattooed beauty, Alexis," the dude with the microphone said from a table at the edge of the room.

Alexis was an interesting case. She had no noticeable tattoos, but there were two quite large tats covering her breasts. There was no detail, and they were the color of her own skin, and the artist had somehow created the illusion that she had no breasts. Once you got within reach (NOT THAT YOU COULD TOUCH), however, it was obvious her protuberances were quite large indeed. It was wild.

"Hey yo, more peanuts over here!" came a shout from

a few tables over.

"I just gave you peanuts!" came the annoying high-pitched voice of the waitress.

"Then somebody's been eating my peanuts!"

"...Thank you Alexis, and next to the stage, the...um...interesting... Donna!"

Donna came to the stage, hauling her tits around like a couple of wet mules; dragging on the ground, literally. And by literally, I don't mean figuratively. Her specialty was tying her bazoombas in a knot. And she didn't just have one knot in her repertoire, either. She could do knots that would make a boy scout blush. I'm talking double sheet bend, trucker's hitch, clove hitch, double fisherman's knot, timber hitch, the list went on and on. By the tenth knot or so, Jimmy had gotten tired of the show. With tits that long, there were hundreds of other things she could do with them, but no, just knots.

"Could I please get some more peanuts?" Came a more polite request for nuts.

"You too?" said the waitress. "I just filled your bowl."

"Somebody's been eating *my* peanuts."

"Hey, mine too!" shouted someone else. "And they ate 'em all up!"

Hmm. There was something about this situation that seemed familiar to Jimmy, and it wasn't old Knotty Tits up on stage. It was food related. Perhaps the person that was stealing everyone's peanuts was the same one who stole the *gabagool*. Or maybe there was an elephant in the room.

A large trunk slithered its way over his shoulder, down his chest, and over to his table grabbing a peanut. As a matter of fact, there *was* an elephant in the room. Every Freaky Friday there was some sort of circus animal there, to add to the overall theme. Jimmy wasn't sure how Myron, the owner of the bar, could afford such exotic animals. He was contemplating this when a shout came from backstage. "Hey, watch it! Hey Charlie, somebody just touched my tits!"

"Watch the tit touching, there," the man with the microphone said.

"Shoo, elephant. Go on, git!" The elephant was determined, however, to eat the peanuts. Still, there's no way he could have eaten as many peanuts as the customers claimed. Somebody else must have been eating the...

"Somebody just touched my tits, too," another voice came from back stage.

"Sir and/or madam, I will ask you one more time nicely to...hey, somebody's touching my tits, too. And here she comes, onstage now, the gorgeous, can't-believe-she's-legal blond from parts unknown, Marguerite!

There she was, walking onto the stage. That little bitch. Jimmy looked at her body as she started taking off articles of clothing, her eyes locked on him the entire time. There was nothing really freaky about her, so he wasn't sure what she was doing here on this night of all nights, but...woah. Okay, *that* was freaky. Jimmy had never seen anyone do *that* before. He looked away in embarrassment, as he knew damn well she was underage.

When her act finished, she clumsily gathered up the dollar bills that the customers had thrown onto the stage, walked off, and took a seat at Jimmy's table.

"Hey," she said.

"Hey," he said. "Look, if you're gonna sit here, put some clothes on or somethin'."

She gave a fake pout. "What's the matter? Don't like what you see?"

"Oh, for the love of...How'd you even get in here?

Aren't you like, a teenager or somethin'?"

"Seventeen."

"Don't you have to be twenty-one in this state?"

She laughed. "You think anyone gives a shit?"

"Probably not. So anyways, what do you want from me?"

"I want to be friends."

"Ha!"

"What's so funny?" she asked.

"You wanna be friends, huh?"

"Yeah. Friends."

"We can't be friends. We'll never be friends."

"Why not?"

"Do you even know who I am?" he asked.

"Of course I know who you are. Everyone knows who you are."

"Then I ask again, what do you want from me?"

"Why did you call the cops on me?"

He laughed. "Is that it? You wanna know why I called the cops? You broke into my house!"

"So? I didn't steal anything from you. Except a few beers and some salami."

"*Gabagool.*"

"Whatever."

"Anyway, it's not about the stealin'. You can't go around breakin' into houses."

"Why not?" she asked.

He couldn't believe he was sitting here having this conversation with a completely naked teenager. "Are you serious right now?"

"Yes. Why can't I do whatever I want? *You* can."

"I don't do whatever I want. In life, there are rules we all have to follow. If you don't follow them, then you gotta learn from your mistakes. That's why I called the cops."

"Oh, like you ever learn from your mistakes?"

"You fuckin' kidding me?" He lifted the front of his shirt up so she could see the nasty scar he had on his stomach. "See that? That's a lesson learnt. See those?" He gestured at the scars across all the crooked fingers on his left hand. "I was a lefty before this. Had to have them all sewn back on after some mook cut them off. I learnt a lesson there, too. Can't even bend these two fingers. See that?"

"Wow, you must have done something horrible to warrant that."

"Not *that* horrible. That mook crossed the line on that one. And so, he learnt his own lesson shortly thereafter."

"Tell me more about that."

"Well see, what happened was... heyyy, wait a minute. You're not gonna get me to talk just 'cause I had a few bourbons. I'm a pro at keepin' my mouth shut.

"And so you killed him, right? No big deal, right? Did it make you feel better?"

"Not really. That's not what it's about. And anyway," he winked, "I didn't kill nobody."

She wondered if a double negative could ever be considered a confession.

"Anyway, you see what I'm gettin' at, right? And jail? You're all bent out of shape over spending one night in jail? You think I ain't been to jail? Ha!"

"And you're still doing what you've always done."

"Yes, but I learnt from it. I'm smarter now. I don't fall asleep on people's couches."

"Good to know. I hear your kid got kicked out of school. Following in his old dad's footsteps?"

"How did you hear that?"

"Never mind how. I know more about you than you think."

"For your information, he wasn't kicked out. We pulled him out. He's goin' to St. Mark's."

"Oh, well isn't that cute? He can hang out with all the other mob kids. What he hasn't already learned from you he can learn from them."

"Keep your voice down."

"Or what?!" she shouted.

"For the third time," said Jimmy, "what do you want from me? You here to blackmail me? Is that it?"

"Hmm, I never thought of that," Blondie said. "You got something I can use?"

"Clean as a whistle."

"Hahahaha. That's a riot." She headed out the door, then turned and shouted to him. This was her signature move. "Catch you on the flip!" she said, and left.

He laughed. She forgot her clothes. Something was not right with this chick. As of now, she was just a kid with maybe a screw or two loose. She was annoying him, but it was nothing to have her whacked over. He needed to be careful of her, though. She reeked of trouble.

10. Meatballs

He checked his watch. Ten o'clock. The night was still young, and he wasn't tired at all. He should probably go to Stella and get some more work done. Also, for some reason, he was feeling frisky. It wasn't the knot girl, or the vanishing tit girl. It wasn't the elephant, and it *certainly* wasn't Blondie. It was most likely the bourbon. Chances are Charlene was already in bed, curled up with a good book, or maybe even sound asleep. Either way, he wasn't getting any tonight. He dialed his phone.

"Hello?"

"Hey, Joe. What's happenin'?"

"Ah, nothin'. At my ma's house. She thought she heard a noise. Come to find out it was just my father fallin' down the steps again."

"Again? What is that, the third time this year?"

"Third time this *month*. I think she pushes him and neither one remembers 'cause they're both so fuckin' senile. Anyway, I was just about to head home. What's up?"

"I was just at Freaky Friday at the Iguana."

"I see. And now you wanna fuck, right?"

"Shh. Not so loud! Your parents!"

"My parents? They are so out of it they don't know what the fuck is going on. Listen to this... Hey ma! I'm gonna go fuck Jimmy in the ass at the club. You wanna join?"

In the background, he heard Joe's mother say: "Take him some meatballs!"

"See what I mean, Jimmy? Anyway, you want some

meatballs?"

"I just ate so much at the Iguana, I don't think I can eat one more bite." After a second's pause, he said, "Bring 'em anyway; you never know."

"Ten-four," Joe said.

"Tin foil?" Jimmy heard Joe's dad shout. "Who's the tin foil man?"

"See you in thirty," Joe said.

Jimmy sat behind his desk in the office, trying to get more paperwork done. Usually a few drinks helped him through the monotony of this process, but tonight he had too many to be able to concentrate. He looked at his watch again. Joe wasn't late yet, but Jimmy was getting anxious nevertheless. He went to the bar and got another bourbon to help calm his nerves and settle his sausage a little.

A knock knock at the door, followed by the door opening, followed by a verbal "knock knock." It was Joe, carrying a tray of meatballs.

"Jesus, Joe, you ain't gotta knock. Also, you ain't gotta say *knock knock*. Makes you sound like a fag."

"Ha. Coming from the man who sucks the best dick this side of the Mason-Dixon."

"Hey, watch it. Next time I just might bite it off."

"Ooh, promises promises," Joe said in a femmey voice.

"All right, quit talkin' in a femmey voice. And lock the door, will ya?"

He locked the door, turned around, and dropped his drawers.

"Nothin' like gettin' down to business, hey, Joe?"

"I gotta be home by midnight or the wife gets pissy," Joe said.

"Who's runnin' the show at your house, anyway?"

"Heh heh. You know the answer to that one. I'm just happy she hasn't noticed me coming home smelling like your cock."

"Okay, less talkin' and more fuckin'."

And they did. For ten really solid minutes, they had some nasty man-on-bear action.

"Ah, ah, ah, AAAAHHH MEATBALLS!" Jimmy shouted as he came.

"Shh, that's wicked loud."

"Sorry," said Jimmy. "These are some really good meatballs!" he yelled as a cover, just in case someone else heard him coming. Also, they *were* good meatballs, he was thinking as he ate a couple. Not as good as Charlene's, but damn good.

"So," Joe said as he zipped up, "catch me up on all that's been goin' on. What's the deal with Blondie?"

He had told Joe a little of the Blondie story previously, but now he told him everything: The popping up in random places, the stripping, the feeling that she was up to something.

"Maybe she is up to somethin'," Joe suggested, as he munched on a meatball.

"Yeah, but what?"

"Dunno. Maybe she's tryin' to blackmail you or somethin'."

"She said she just wanted to be friends. That was all. Besides, she ain't got nothin' on me to blackmail me with."

Joe laughed heartily.

"What?" Jimmy asked.

"Are you nuts? Did you forget who you were for a second? Did you fall down a flight of stairs and bump your head? You're as bad as my mom and dad for Chrissakes. Someone could pull up a whole bunch of things on you if they dug hard enough."

"Get real," he said as he munched. "She ain't that bright," Jimmy said. "Plus, she said she don't want nothin' from me. She's got money, and I don't know what else she'd want."

"Well, it's gotta be somethin'. Believe me, with females, it's always somethin'."

And Joe was right. It was something. And there, in the supply closet, between the reams of paper and boxes of staples, there was a ship in a bottle that Jimmy had built. And there, in that ship in a bottle, was a small camera that a blond girl had planted in there when no one was looking.

And there, at home in her bedroom, sitting on her computer, a mischievous grin on her face, Blondie was watching the whole thing.

11. Gabagool

"Got you, you sonofabitch," she said.

She hit stop, saved the video as a file, and made a copy on a thumb drive. She had him right where she wanted him, now. She could do anything, *anything*, with the file, and in one way or another he would be completely ruined.

The question was, what *should* she do with it? Should she leave it for Jimmy's wife to see? Surely that would be the end of their relationship. His family, the most important thing in life to him, would be destroyed in a matter of minutes. She could just imagine the look on his wife's face as she watched him plowing his best friend from behind. Her husband. A, what did they call it? *Fanook?* Her husband, a *fanook*. What a riot! She'd take the boy and leave. Or better yet, she'd kick him out of his own house and take him for everything he had. But was that the worst thing that could happen to him? It was terrible, certainly, but she didn't think it was the worst thing. His wife may divorce him, but she may also be the type of person to keep it a secret, and just make up some other story as to why she kicked him out. For one, she could be a kind-hearted woman who didn't want to see Jimmy humiliated. And her husband fooling around on her with another man? *She'd* also be humiliated, and the boy would be scarred for life, and Charlene wouldn't want that.

She could send it to Charlene's dad, the real head of the

family. Jimmy would lose his job for sure. And in the mafia, there was really only one way to lose your job. You either fled and ended up in witness protection, or you stopped breathing. She knew the old man wouldn't give Jimmy a chance to run, so that left the other option. For sure he'd cease to exist, but again, she didn't think that was the worst thing. Most likely, the old man would kill him mercifully and blame it on a rival. She knew how the mob worked. Jimmy had done a lot of good things for the Family, brought in a lot of wealth and moved up their status as a force to be reckoned with. And the one indiscretion, however large it may seem, was outweighed by all the good he did. No, his death would be quick and painless. He needed to die, for sure, but before that happened, he needed to be shamed. He needed his world to come crashing down around him before he was offed. And when he was shamed, the entire Family would be shamed. Then his death wouldn't be so quick and painless. Bringing embarrassment to the Family was the worst thing that could be done. His father-in-law would be devastated. He would have no choice but to set an example of Jimmy just to save face. It would be incredible. He would be shamed, then tortured, then killed. This had to become a scandal. But how?

She needed to brainstorm. Perhaps a little weed would help her mind think more clearly. She fired up her volcano vaporizer, filled the plastic bag with weed vapor, and inhaled the whole thing in one in-breath. She'd never taken the whole bag in like that, and it instantly made her head dizzy. She lay down and closed her eyes.

She wasn't sure if what she saw was a dream or not, but she envisioned herself lost in the woods. She was tired, hungry, and thirsty, and was about to give up, when she saw a cabin in the distance. When she got up to it, she found the door was locked, so she took a rock and threw it through a window. She climbed inside. She was really in the mood for some capicola, but there was no fridge to be found. Instead, what she found were three bowls of what appeared to be porridge resting on the counter. This reminded her of her time in jail. She tried the first bowl, which was too hot. The next bowl was too cold and congealed, like wallpaper paste. Although she did enjoy the taste of a good wallpaper paste, this was worse. She moved onto the third bowl, which was exactly the right temp, which didn't make sense. It should have been the coldest of the three, as it was the smallest bowl and thus should have cooled off faster. Regardless, she knew that's how the story went, so who was she to argue?

She was right in the middle of the most thermally pleasing of the three bowls of porridge (which, incidentally, still tasted like shit), when she heard keys rattling in the front door's lock. She quickly scanned the cabin for a place to hide, but it was very open concept, as most fabled cabins in the woods tended to be. She was doomed.

In barged a giant bear with gold chains and a nice suit. *Gabagool!* he shouted. The mother bear walked in behind him. *Gabagool!* she screamed. The baby bear was the last to enter, and when he saw her still eating his food, he shouted, *Gabagool! Haha!* His dad said, pointing at him. *Private school!*

Private school. That's it. Oh, thank you to the gods of weed, they gave her the answer she had been looking for. She knew just where to send the thumb drive. This was gonna be good.

12. St. Mark's

Sister Mary Josephine, St. Mark's resident professor of Calculus and New Testament studies, as well as the founder of Stigmata Awareness Month, went through the daily mail. Amongst all the propaganda from the Church of Scientology (who the hell added them to their mailing list, she'd never know) and Applebee's coupons, there was a small manila envelope. She opened it up, and a thumb drive fell out with a note: PLAY ME.

Fearing that something Satanic was hidden within, and therefore not wanting to touch it, she went to the office and knocked on Father Healy's door. At this point, I could do the cliché thing, and make a joke about how there was a boy with no trousers in his office, but that would be crass and frankly a joke that has been overplayed for the last twenty years. Not only that, abuse in the Catholic church is a very serious issue that shouldn't be taken lightly, and is nothing to laugh about. So I will only mention *in passing* that there was a boy with no trousers in his office, rather than make the usual joke.

"Father Healy?"

"What is it, Sister?"

"We just received something in the mail that may or may not be very disturbing and I think you should take a look at it."

"I'll be right there. Hold that pose, Jeremy," he told the

boy, and went into the hall, shutting the door behind him.

He looked at the pile of mail, and the thumb drive cast off to the side, along with the note.

"What do you think it is?" he asked.

"It's a thumb drive," Sister Mary Josephine said.

"No shit. I mean, what do you think is on it?"

"Beats me. It may be something Satanic."

"Or worse," he said. "It could be Scientologic."

She shuddered at that thought. "Come to think of it, there was an unusual amount of Scientology propaganda in the mail today. Who put us on all these mailing lists?"

"I have no idea. I tried to cancel the subscriptions, but then I received a letter in the mail stating that I would be labeled a Suppressive Person and would be forever considered an enemy of the Church, and then Kirstie Alley would stop my Jenny Craig subscription. And we can't have that."

"Come to think of it, you have slimmed down lately."

"Thank you. You know, Jeremy was just saying the same thing? Come on, let's see what's on this thing."

"Wait!" Sister Mary Josephine said in fear. "Don't pop it in just yet!"

"You know," Father Healy said, "Jeremy was just saying the same thing."

Sorry.

They put the thumb drive in the nearest computer and opened it. There was only one file in there, named JDF. Father Healy double-clicked on the file, and Windows Media Player opened up to play the filthiest video he'd ever seen. Well, it wasn't the *filthiest* video he'd ever seen, let's get real; not even close. However, it was the worst horror Sister Mary Josephine had ever witnessed, and she'd seen quite a few exorcisms as well as Leah Remini's documentary on Scientology.

"God," she blasphemed, "it's terrible. Turn it off, please!"

He was about to, but instead said, "Wait."

"For what?" she asked desperately.

"We were sent this for a reason. We need to watch the whole thing through." Plus, this was giving him a slight erection, which was more than he could say for Jeremy.

I said I'm sorry!

There was something about this video, other than the fact that it was turning him on. Specifically, something about the man in the back. He looked familiar to him.

"Sister, does the man standing up look at all familiar to you?"

"I can't see!" she said, as she had covered her own eyes.

Father Healy paused the video and covered up the bottom half of the screen with his hand. "Okay, now look."

"Oh my God."

"Sister! Language!"

"Sorry. I meant oh, *fuck*!"

"Who is that man?" Healy asked.

"That, sir, is Jimmy DiFrenzo."

"Oh, shit!"

"Double shit. You just enrolled his boy here."

"Oh no! Well, *that* was a mistake, certainly. We can't have that. We need to notify the family right away. His boy can't come here. Not after this."

"This is a big deal," Sister Mary Josephine said.

"This is a *gigantic* deal," Healy echoed.

Now, even though the Catholic church had put their foot down on priests and little boys, they had loosened their stance on homosexuality in general; especially ever since what the whole world had deemed the "cool pope" had been elected. The fact that little Jimmy DiFrenzo's father was gay had no bearing on his son going there. Or rather, it wouldn't have had any bearing if Jimmy Senior was open about it.

Blackmailing the man was out of the question. There were countless examples throughout history of those who attempted to blackmail someone in the mob, with no good outcomes from any of them. He would have to go with the next best thing: Selling the story. Father Healy would expose this scandal for all it was worth, and he would make sure to get every dime he could out of it. It would mean lots of money for the church, as well as whatever he deemed fair to skim off the top.

"Call the papers, Sister," he said. "We're gonna be rich!"

13. Awfully Sorry

Charlene's cell phone rang.

"Hello?"

"Hi, Mrs. DiFrenzo, this is Father Healy from St. Mark's. How are you today?"

"Oh, hi, Father. Just fine, thank you. How are you?"

"I'm okay, thanks. I was wondering if you and/or your husband had any time tomorrow where we could meet up for coffee and discuss some things."

"Gee, I wish we could, Father. But I have a lot going on this weekend, and my husband has his work, you know."

"His...work. Right."

"Is everything okay?" she asked. "Can we talk about it Monday when we come sign the paperwork?"

"Well, uh, that's what I wanted to talk to you about. I really didn't want to do this over the phone. You see, after much review and deliberation, uh it seems we, uh, we can't accept Jimmy here after all."

"WHAT?" she shouted.

"What's going on?" Jim Sr. called up from the basement when he heard her shout. He had been tinkering down there, fixing the auger in his snowblower. Sure, there were months to go before the snow fell, but, dear friends, if you get nothing else out of this book, heed these words: Test your snowblower before winter hits. You don't want to be stuck in a storm without a working snowblower.

"Father Healy said they can't take Jimmy," she yelled to him.

He raced up the stairs. "What are you talking about?"

"They can't take Jimmy," she said through her tears.

"Gimme that." He grabbed the phone out of her hand.

"Hi, Father? James DiFrenzo here."

"Hi, Mr. DiFrenzo."

"What's this about you can't take my son?"

"I'm very sorry," Father Healy said.

"Fuck!"

"Jim!" Charlene scolded.

"Sorry, Father," he said.

"It's quite all right. I know this probably comes as a shock to you. I just wanted to let you know as quickly as I could, before you pulled him out of public school."

"That's already done," Jimmy said.

"I'm sorry to hear that," Father Healy said. "I'm sure they'll take him back. They have to. It's a public school, after all."

"Why the change, suddenly?"

"I can't really disclose why at the moment."

"Bullshit!"

"Jim!" Charlene scolded again.

"No! I have a right to know. You can't just reject my son without lettin' me know why. What did he do?"

"It's nothing he did. Believe me. As I said, I can't disclose the reason right now, but rest assured you will know as soon as humanly possible. I just wanted to make sure Jimmy had the opportunity to stay in school before he fell too far behind. Good day, Mr. DiFrenzo."

The line went dead. Jimmy dialed the number that the call came from, but it went straight to voice mail.

"Son of a bitch," Jimmy said.

Charlene blew her nose into an old grocery receipt, as they were out of tissues. It never occurred to her that she could use toilet paper. Grocery store receipts were not known for their absorbency, as they were not intended to be used to mop up messes on the kitchen counter or absorb mucus, so the snot made a white and yellow messy streak all over her mouth and cheeks.

"Oh, Jimmy. What did our boy do this time?"

"Our boy? Our boy did nothin'. Just a bunch of fucked-up politics, is all. They don't want to let us in because they know what I do for a living. You got a little somethin' there," Jimmy said, and he wiped Charlene's face with his handkerchief.

"Honey, that makes no sense. Half the children in there are just like our son. There has to be another reason."

Oh yeah, there *was* another reason. He just knew it. That blond-headed bitch was behind all this. He wasn't sure how, but one way or another he was going to get to the bottom of it.

Right on cue, his phone rang.

"Hello?" he answered.

"Hi Jimmy! It's me!"

That fucking she-devil had the nerve to call him. How did she get his number? *Nobody* outside of his family, and his other family, had his number. Also, what perfect timing. It's almost as though she knew that he had just been talking to the school. Did she have his house bugged? His phone tapped? What was her deal? She needed to go, there was no doubt in his mind. She *had* to, or she'd continue fucking with him forever. He wasn't sure why she had it in for him so badly; just because she spent a night in jail? Get over it. It wasn't a big deal, and he was planning on dropping the charges. She didn't know that, but still. She had it out for him, and it occurred to him that that meant the same as having it *in* for him. Same as calling *out* sick versus calling *in* sick. They mean the same thing too. It makes no sense to me, and it made no sense to him. His head was boiling. It had all been harmless up to this point, but now she had gone too far. Something she did had messed with his son's education. She needed to die.

"Oh, hi," he answered jovially. He couldn't let on that he was going to kill her, or that he suddenly learned that *in* and *out* could mean the same thing. Best to keep it casual.

"I gotta take this," he said to Charlene.

She nodded. She knew what that meant. Business call.

"What's going on?" she asked. Was that a giggle?

"Just got off the phone with St. Mark's. They can't take Jimmy."

"Oh. So sorry to hear that," she said. He knew fake sincerity when he heard it. He was surrounded by it all the time, from practically everyone he knew. Even Joe, at times. But it was best to just play into her bullshit, for now.

"Hey, I was just thinkin' about you," he said.

"Oh, really?" said Blondie.

"Really. You know, I've been thinkin'. I'm gonna drop the breakin' and enterin' charges."

"Why?" she asked.

"What do you mean *why*? I thought you'd be happy about it."

"Oh, I am," she said. "I'm just wondering why the sudden change of heart."

"Remember that speech I gave last night, about how I learnt my lessons by going to jail?"

"Vividly."

"Yeah, well, it ain't true. I haven't learnt shit."

"No?"

"No. I just learnt how to be more crafty and not get caught. Didn't make me a more law-abiding citizen. In fact, just the opposite."

"I know. I mean, it's obvious."

"I guess I just wanted to teach you not to mess with me, is all."

"Duly noted."

"The more I thought about it, though, the more I realized, people don't respond to punishment as nice as they do to kindness. And I know everyone thinks the contrary, but I do have a good heart."

"Sure," she said.

"That's why I want to give you a college education. So you can make somethin' of yourself."

"Wait, what? Give me a college education? You're gonna teach me?"

"No. I'm gonna pay for your school. I wanna see you on the right track. Anywhere you wanna go, name it, and it's yours."

"Oh, Jimmy, I can't accept that. Besides, my mom can afford it."

"It ain't about affordin' it. You *can* accept it and you *will*. Case closed. One stipulation."

"What's that?"

"No more breaking into houses."

"Consider it done."

"Also, I ain't payin' for a liberal arts degree or women's studies. I don't wanna see you workin' at Dick's Sportin' Goods when you graduate. Anyways, what's up?"

"You know," she said, "I forgot why I called."

"That's okay. I'm glad you did. What are you doing tomorrow, around lunch time?" he asked coyly.

"Nothing that I know of," she answered, also coyly.

"How 'bout I take you out to lunch tomorrow, at Rossi's, my treat?" he asked. *And then I'll murder you,* he thought.

"Sounds great," she said. *And then I'll murder you,* she thought.

He looked down at his shirt and found a slice of bread left over from dinner stuck to it. Friggin' bread. Always landing butter-side down. He pulled it off like a soggy Band-Aid, dunked it in some sauce that had fallen on his lap, and stuffed it in his yapper. Mmmm, nothing like leftovers!

"Sho," he said through a mouthful of gluten, "She you tomarrah, eleven firty."

"Right on," she said, and hung up the phone. "You fat fucking pig," she added.

14. I Don't Know But I Don't Feel So Good

She sat on the edge of her bed, running her hands along the smooth surface of her Glock, not knowing how to feel. She *should* feel thrilled, instead she felt nervous. He really deserved torture, like, a *lot* of it. But she didn't have it in her. A quick bullet to the head would have to suffice. She had no idea what she was doing. She had never even shot a gun before. Why in the hell did she think this was going to work? She was going to fail at this like she did everything else.

Calm down, Marguerite, don't overthink it. Just go meet him tomorrow, and if the time seems right, if there's no one around, aim, click, boom. Simple. If not, try again when the scenario seems better. He has to be caught off-guard. And absolutely no witnesses, or you, my dear, are fucked.

She needed to stop worrying about it; right now she should probably get some sleep. It was getting late, and she should be as well-rested as possible for the next day.

...Which came sooner than she wanted. She didn't get any sleep the night before. Her head was spinning like she was hung over, but she hadn't had anything to drink the night before; this was just sheer exhaustion.

It was only eight in the morning. There was time to have a couple of cups of coffee before she even made an effort at starting to get ready. She opened the pantry door to get the coffee, and discovered there were no filters. "Ugh," she said in frustration. She tore a paper towel off the roll and attempted to fold it so it would fit in the basket. Try as she might, though, she couldn't get it into the shape she needed.

Come on, Blondie, you've done this before. You can make it work.

On the first attempt at folding, she made a swan. On the second attempt, a frog. On the third attempt, a bust of Beethoven. But for some reason, folding a square into a triangle was baffling her. Finally, she crumpled it into a ball, threw some coffee grounds on it, and turned it on. She'd let that brew while she took a shower.

The shower did nothing to wake her up. And after chewing on three cups of coffee grounds, she was still just as tired. *Maybe another hour of sleep,* she thought, and headed back to bed to toss and turn for sixty minutes before giving up.

She felt worse. It felt like someone beat her with a shoe. Maybe she was getting mono or the flu or something. Briefly, she contemplated calling Jimmy and telling him she couldn't make it. Very briefly. Terrible idea. She had a feeling that he had a feeling that she was up to something. She couldn't quite put her finger on it, but there was something suspicious in the way he sounded on the phone. If she called him up and canceled, it might piss him off. It was best to play it cool and keep the lunch date.

She got up out of bed and was struck by a wave of dizziness. She glanced at the clock. Quarter past ten. Time to get ready. One quick glance in the mirror told her she needed to put on a lot of makeup. There weren't just dark circles under her eyes, there were dark circles all around her eyes. It looked like she got in a bar fight with a Korean delivery boy.

    Eleven o'clock. Time to head out. She picked her Glock up off the bed, opened her desk drawer, placed it in gently, and closed it. Today was not the day for murder.

15. I Don't Know What You Mean, I Feel Great!

He sat on the edge of his bed, running his hands along the smooth surface of his Smith and Wesson Model 19. He was excited to get this over with. Blondie really deserved to be tortured for sure. He wasn't convinced he wanted to waste the time and effort it took to do that, though. He may just put a quick bullet in her head. Priority was getting rid of her. She just needed to be gone. She wasn't a physical threat, but he had no idea what that unstable little bitch was capable of. She already got his boy kicked out of school before he even began. But how? Could it be that he was wrong? Maybe it wasn't her, after all. If only they'd told him over the phone what happened. Should he wait till he found out the reason? They told him he would know soon enough. But what if she pulled something else in the meantime? She was horrible, vindictive, and needed to be stopped. Now.

Just go meet her tomorrow, Jimmy, and if the time seems right, if there's no one around, aim, click, boom. Simple. If not, try again when the scenario seems better. She has to be caught off-guard. And no witnesses.

Anyway, it was getting late and he needed to get his rest for tomorrow. "You coming to bed, Charl?" he yelled down the stairs.

"Be up in a bit," she yelled up.

And later on she would be. It wasn't often she went to bed after him, but when she did, she had the ability to slip in unnoticed, without waking him up. So he decided to put the gun on the dresser. He didn't want to fall asleep with it in bed and have it accidentally go off and shoot Charlene in the face.

He woke up feeling great. It was eight in the morning. Plenty of time to have a couple of cups of coffee before he needed to start getting his day rolling. He opened the pantry door. Which coffee should he start the day off with today? Ahh, yes. French roast. His favorite. But don't tell the other guys that. Real Italians drink espresso. He put the filter in the basket, put the grounds in the filter, hit ON, and it started its drip. He was falling right into stride today.

While that was going, it was time for his shower. It sure felt nice. Today he even decided to scrub behind his ears and in his belly button. Plus, he washed his feet, for the first time *ever*. I mean, who does that? Standing in the soapy water was usually enough, but not for Jimmy. Not today. He wanted to be extra clean for the special occasion.

He didn't think it was possible to feel any better, but dammit if the shower didn't make him even more happy and upbeat than he was when he first got up. "Plenty of sunshine headin' my way," he sang as he poured himself a cup of coffee in the nude.

"Hey dad," little Jimmy said, as he gazed at his dad's little Jimmy.

"Zippity doo dah, zippity ay!" he continued to sing as he sipped his coffee and skipped merrily down the hall and back up the stairs.

"Mr. bluebird on my shoulder," Junior could hear all the way in the kitchen. He didn't know why his dad was in such a good mood, especially after the news he got last night.

Jimmy Senior was in a good mood, even after the news he got last night. He was always in high spirits when he was going to kill someone. Today was a day for murder!

Now fully clothed, he stepped outside onto the porch to get the morning paper. The paperboy had thrown it high into the tree. That was okay, though. Nothing could spoil his mood today. That is, until he got it down from the tree and looked at the front page. The headline read MOB BOSS OUT! Underneath it was his photo. He had never directly made the front page of the paper. Nothing good could come from this. And right next to his bulbous head, was Joe's head. Jimmy looked like he was shouting, and Joe looked like he was in agony. When he unfolded the paper to see the bottom half of the photo, he saw his own bottom half. As well as Joe's. There he was, plowing away at Joe's ass like an overzealous cowboy at an Irish rodeo. His first thought, he never realized his ass was that hairy. He never had much of an opportunity to look at it. His second thought, once reality hit, was that it appeared as though he was shouting "MEATBALLS!" And that's because he was. He remembered it clearly. It was the last time he and Joe had fucked. In his office at the club. All of a sudden he felt dizzy. He needed to go lie down for a while. He didn't even make it through his front door when the lights went out in his head and he passed out on the porch.

"Hey, Dad," he heard his son's voice say.

"Nothing, you?" That didn't make sense. He was out of it. But not so out of it that he didn't have the good sense to stuff the paper underneath his body. That was the last thing he needed his son to see.

Doesn't matter, though, does it? It's in the papers! He's gonna know anyway!

"Shut up! Just shut your mouth!"

"What did I say?" Junior asked.

"Sorry. Go get your mother."

He turned to go.

"No! Wait! Don't get your mother. Just, um, I'll be okay. Really."

"All right," said Junior. "I wasn't really asking."

"Never mind! Go play!"

"I'm hungry. Can I eat some cereal?"

"Yes! Eat some cereal! Go eat!"

Junior turned to go again.

"Wait! What time is it?"

"It's ten forty-five, Dad."

"Ten forty-five? Oh shit. That stupid blond whore is behind this. That bitch is gonna die today. She's *gotta* die."

"Who?" asked Junior.

"Did I say that out loud? I thought I thought it."

"You're scaring me. I'm gonna go get mom."

"No!" He jumped up, still a little dizzy, but not too dizzy to run to his Hummer and burn rubber out of there. He checked the glove box. The Glock was in there. It wasn't the Smith and Wesson he'd hoped to use today, but it would have to do.

16. The Back Room

He was halfway to the restaurant when he realized he'd forgotten to grab the paper from the porch on his way out. Charlene! It was too late to turn back. If Junior would have just let her sleep instead of rushing in to wake her up, he probably would have turned around. At this point, however, he had to keep pushing onward.

His cell phone rang violently. He didn't have to look at the screen to know who it was. Charlene. Right on cue. He hit the IGNORE button. He didn't want to give her the opportunity to leave a voice mail. He would have been too tempted to listen to it while he was sitting there waiting for Blondie.

This was it. He was ruined. He would lose his family over this. His wife may have forgiven him over having a *goomah*, but he doubted it highly. And his *goomah* being a dude? There was no mercy for that one. She would kick him out and never let him see his child again. There was the hope that she wouldn't tell her father. But of course she would tell her father. Jimmy would be ruined. Literally. His only other option was to run. But Don would find him eventually. The old man had his ways.

He pulled up across the street from Rossi's and watched the door so Blondie couldn't go in without him.

His phone vibrated. A text.
WHAT THE FUCK???

Three question marks from Charlene. It was worse than he had expected. There was nothing he could do at this point.

The phone vibrated again.

CALL ME!!! Said another text. There was no way he was going to do that. He had nothing to say. No explanations. No excuses. He was a cheat, plain and simple. No way he was going to talk his way out of it.

Another vibration.

UR A FUCKING ASSHOLE!!!!!!!!!

Enough! Jimmy set the phone on the center console and rammed his fist through it. It didn't take much to break the screen, but he kept on punching it. Over and over until there was nothing left but small particles and lots of blood. He was normally one to keep his cool, he had to be, but at that moment he just lost it.

He *was* a fucking asshole. No denying it.

It was time to pull himself together, now. He'd had his outburst, now he needed to clean up and get ready for Blondie to come pulling up. He opened the center console and found some McDonald's napkins to wipe up his hand with. There was half a bottle of scotch in there as well. Probably not as good for cleaning wounds as, say, vodka or gin, with all its impurities, but it would have to do. He poured it on his hand, and it hurt like a motherfucker. Good. He deserved it. The more it hurt, the better.

Blondie pulled up in her car and got out. She didn't look well at all. What was that look? Was she sick? Was that guilt on her face? Well, he was about to find out. He rolled down his window. "Hey," he shouted, "Blondie!"

She turned and did a half-hearted wave.

"Wait up." He ripped up one of his shirts from the back seat, wrapped it around his hand, tucked his gun in his waistband, and got out of the Hummer.

"How you feelin'?" he asked. "You don't look good at all."

"Flu or something. I don't know. Maybe we should reschedule."

"Nonsense," Jimmy said. "You know what they say about the flu? You gotta feed it."

"That's a cold. You're supposed to starve a fever."

"Bah, fevers gotta eat, too. Come on, I've set up something special for us."

"You have?"

"Sure. Shall we?" He opened the door for her and followed her in.

"Welcome, Mr. DiFrenzo!" Alfonso, the owner, greeted him kindly. There was no indication that he'd seen the morning paper. "And who's this lovely lady?"

"This is, uh... um... Blondie."

"Blondie?" Alfonso asked.

"Marguerite," she corrected.

"Ah, Margarita, like the drink. Very spicy!"

"Say, uh," Alfonso whispered in Jimmy's ear, "A little young this time, hey?"

Jimmy just nodded and smiled. "I was wonderin' if you'd let me give her the full tour. You know, show her the back room?"

"The, uh...back...room?" Alfonso said.

"Yeah. The back room. I think she'd like to see it."

Alfonso had let him use the back room before. Several times, in fact, for business purposes. Two would go in, only one would come out. He was always compensated, of course.

He whispered again. "Mr. DiFrenzo, are you sure? You have never taken a lady into the back room before."

"I just thought she'd like it, is all. Come on, honey. Let's go see the back room."

They walked through the dining room. There were a fair amount of patrons, and Jimmy could see some of them staring and whispering to each other; some were even laughing. He wanted to scream *take a fucking picture,* but he needed to keep his cool.

He led her, zombie-like, into the kitchen, through another set of doors and down a long hallway. At the end of the hallway was a blue door.

"After you," he said, shoving her in.

He turned on the light and in the far corner was what resembled an electric chair with straps, covered in the blood of other associates. He led her to it, sat her down, and strapped her in. This was too easy. She wasn't even putting up a fight.

"See, you, little bitch, have been trying to make my life miserable. I didn't know what you were up to, at first. I still don't. But when my boy got kicked out of Catholic school, I knew you had to be behind it somehow. You little fuck, you let the school know my secret, didn't you?"

She nodded slowly.

"That's what I thought. While I appreciate your honesty, you don't get any points for it. Now, this is where it gets fun!" he said excitedly.

"Huh?" she asked, in a daze.

"What's wrong with you, anyways?"

"What's going on?" she asked.

"Shit. You *are* out of it."

He went to the Craftsman rolling tool bench in the corner, and started pulling out power tools. He kept an eye on her, looking for her reaction, but there was none.

Out they came, one by one, electric drill, circular saw,

dynamite, reciprocating saw, nothing. It wasn't until he took the jackhammer out that she made a noise. But it wasn't screaming, or even crying. At first, he thought it was crying, because it was a tad on the hysterical side, but she was laughing. He was going to kill her, torture her, and she's laughing?

"What's so fuckin' funny?" he asked.

"I... I was... ho ho hee.... I was planning... ha ha ha... to kill *you*."

"Kill *me*? Why the fuck would you kill me? I thought you wanted to blackmail me."

"Blackmail you? Why would I blackmail you? I'm rich as fuck; there's nothing I want or need. No, I have been planning to kill you for *years*."

"Why, though? I don't get it," said Jimmy.

"You don't huh? You don't recognize me at all, do you?"

He looked hard at her face. "Can't say I recall."

"Think back. Fifteen years."

"Okay?"

"You killed someone."

"Honey, you're gonna have to get more specific than that."

"Those scars on your hands? The ones you were telling me about the other night?"

"What about 'em?"

"My goddamned *father* did that. And that was my goddamned *father* that you yanked out of his fucking truck and killed in cold blood in the street."

That explained it. "Oh, shit."

"Did you know there was a little girl in the back seat of the cab? Watching the whole fucking thing? I watched it all, you sick fuck. And not a day goes by I don't think about the disgusting shit I saw you do to him. I still get nightmares. I never had the courage to approach you, let alone plan to kill you, but the other night I had a nightmare that was so bad it made my fucking skin crawl just to picture your fat fucking face."

She spit on him. He felt the wad dangle from his chin but didn't bother to wipe it away. He was too busy contemplating what to do.

"Contemplating what to do?" she asked.

He didn't answer.

"Go ahead. Kill me. Get it over with already. I was going to take my own life anyway, after I killed you. Life is fucking boring, and if the only thing that provides relief from the boredom is the nightmares, I can do without it."

Well, when she put it that way, it made sense. She was in pain because of him. No wonder she hated him so much. He supposed he could do her a favor and end her life. He wasn't going to make her suffer, though. After a lifetime of torture, she deserved a quick end. He screwed the silencer on his pistol, aimed the gun at her wincing face, and fired.

17. Don Figarazzi

Jimmy got himself a hotel room that day. He couldn't face his family, that was for sure. His life was finished. At least here he may be able to buy himself a couple days before he met a fate similar to Blondie's. The mini bar was well-stocked in the room, so he cracked a couple of little bottles, turned the t.v. on, and tried to relax.

Around three p.m. the phone in his room rang.

"Hello?"

"Meet me at the docks. Six o'clock."

Don Figarazzi. Jimmy knew he would be found eventually, but he didn't think it would be this quick. The old man never ceased to amaze him. This is why he couldn't run. Don was good.

It was half past four. He couldn't take it anymore. This may have been the shortest wait on death row in history, but it felt like an eternity. The wait was killing him. Jimmy needed to leave now. He'd track Don down and end it on the spot. He chugged a couple more mini bottles, got in his vehicle, and headed to the docks.

18. The Docks

Jimmy pulled up to the docks a little past five. Some shady guys were unloading some shady ships of shady merchandise, shadily. Looked like it was business as usual. Most of the guys were whispering, gesturing, and laughing, much like at the restaurant. He knew most of the boys here, and he didn't stop to chat, or to yell and scream. He headed straight for Don's office. It didn't matter if Don was in the middle of something. He would make him deal with him right then and there. Nothing was that important that it couldn't wait.

Jimmy barged right into Don's office; there was no need for propriety at this point. Except Don wasn't there. It was someone else. "Hey, Jimmy."

"Joe? The fuck you doin' here?" Jimmy asked. Then it dawned on him what he was most likely there for. Don wanted to have a "talk" with Joe as well. But why would Don want to kill Joe before he killed *him*? Shouldn't killing Jimmy be the first order of business? Was Don trying to say that Joe was more important than him? He glared at Joe, suddenly disgusted with him. What was that on his face?

"You got a little somethin' there," Jimmy said.

Joe wiped his face.

"No, no. On your chin." He got out his napkin and wiped Joe's chin for him. There was no mistaking the consistency of this glob. It was most definitely semen.

Right on cue, the boss came out of the bathroom, zipping up.

"Don?" Jimmy asked. "What the *fuck*?"

He looked back and forth at his boss and his *goomah* in disbelief.

"You're early," Don said.

"You're fucking my man?" Jimmy yelled at Don.

"No," answered Don. "I'm not."

"Whew," said Jimmy.

"*You're* fucking *my* man."

"Now, wait, Don."

"Now wait nothin'" Don said. "Look, Jimmy, we all got secrets, right? I just keep mine out of the *fucking paper*!" He threw the newspaper at him.

"That wasn't my fault!" Jimmy said.

"Gimme that," Joe said, and grabbed the paper from the floor.

"Oh, shit," Joe said.

"Jimmy, Jimmy, Jimmy," Don said, "You know it's a rule. You don't steal another man's whore." He aimed his gun at Joe. "And you. You cheating piece of shit," he said, and fired. Joe dropped dead.

"And as for you. You're fired. Your cousin Donald is gonna take your place."

"Oh" Jimmy said. "Hold on. Does this mean you're gonna let me go?"

Don shook his head. "No, you're still a dead man," he said. "But you're also fired."

"Oh,"

"See, you brought disgrace to the Family. The whole fuckin' world knows what you did. I can't just let you go. How would it look for me? Plus," said Don, a tear in his eye as he aimed his gun once more, this time at Jimmy's head, "you broke my daughter's heart."

THE END

THE ALPHABET BOOKS: ABC

C is for

Cookie

For those of you in the UK, as I'm sure you know, in the US, our "cookie" is what you folks call a biscuit. Our "biscuits" are more like unsweetened scones. But I already had "B is for Bear" and I wasn't about to do "B is for Biscuit", so you'll just have to get used to my speaking American. I could have done "C is for Crumpet", but around here we call our version "English muffins", which aren't like muffins at all. This actually may be an insult to England, since crumpets are so much better. Plus, this book is about cookies.

1. That's Good Enough for Me

The old man sat in the living room, whittling and watching *Cargo Wars* on the television, only halfway paying attention to the knife as it missed the knob of wood he was working on and flayed his hand wide open. His wife and two grown children laughed heartily as he bled out all over the room, staining the already heavily stained couch.

"Haha, good one, Dad. You did it again!" His twenty-six-year-old boy, Hansel, chuckled.

"Yer dumb!" Said his twenty-four-year-old daughter, Gretel.

His glare said it all. He was not impressed. "Somebody get me a goddamned rag!" The old man yelled.

The wife rushed out of the room, hurrying back with a roll of paper towels.

"I said a rag, you ninny! Something to stop the bleeding!"

"Oh, you'll be fine, dear. This happens every night."

It was true. It happened every night, like clockwork.

"Yet you continue to whittle," the wife said.

It was true. He did continue to whittle every night, like clockwork.

"Why don't you give it up, Dad?" Gretel asked.

"Because," said the father, "It's my job."

"Your job?" asked the wife. "You've been doing this for years and years and you haven't sold one yet. This place just keeps on piling up with your little carvings. Have you seen the spare bedroom lately? We could never have anyone over for drinks and give them a place to sleep. You can't even see the bed. You can barely open the door. It's chock-full of the little nothings you've created. I don't even know what they're supposed to be." She held up the piece he had been working on. "I mean, look at this. What is this?"

"It's a battleship."

"A battleship? It looks, like, the complete opposite of a battleship. If someone asked me to carve the complete opposite of a battleship, this is most likely what I'd come up with. You've been doing this long enough, honey. You should be honing your skill. Instead, you've gotten worse since the beginning."

"That's because I keep cutting myself!" he answered. "I have no feeling in my left hand."

"Maybe you should get a real job, Dad," Hansel suggested.

"Yeah," Gretel agreed.

"Maybe *I* should get a real job? Maybe *I* should get a real job?"

"Yes," said Hansel. "A real job. How do you expect to support us with those shitty wood carvings nobody wants to buy?"

"Support you?" the old man said. "Support you? You're adults! Why am I still trying to support you?"

"'Cause we're your kids, Dad," Gretel said.

"Yeah, well, that's up for debate still." He rolled his eyes at his wife. "Hey, here's a novel idea. Why don't *you two* get jobs?"

Hansel and Gretel looked at each other for a few seconds, then a rather large guffaw escaped the both of them. "Hahaha!" said Hansel. "Funny, Dad. Jobs. Ha!"

"I'm serious. I've had it with trying to support a family of four. When your mother gave birth to you two ingrates,

I was under the impression that after eighteen long years, I'd be done with this shit. Yet here you are, still."

"That's 'cause you love us," Gretel said.

"Yes. I do love you kids. That's why I think it's time you grew up and became respectable members of society."

"But Daaaad..." whined Gretel.

"Don't *but Dad* me. It's high time you made something of yourselves. You should be out there making your mother and me proud. You should be making *you* proud. Don't you want more out of life?"

Brother and sister shook their collective heads. "Not really," they said, in unison.

"You have till the end of the month to get the hell out of my house," said the old man.

"But what are we gonna do?" asked Hansel.

"Yeah," said Gretel. "We have no skills."

A silence fell over them as they all mulled this thought over. It was true. They had no skills. Their attention turned back to the TV, where truck drivers were bidding on long-haul jobs.

"That's it!" yelled the old man, joyfully. "That's what you're gonna do. Long haul trucking!"

The two grown children had another hard laugh.

"I'm serious," the father said.

The silence once again crept in as the children mulled over just how idiotic their father's idea was.

Until the guy with the big beard on TV won his bid to haul a truck full of dwarfs to some broad's castle a thousand miles away. Twenty-six hundred dollars won him the bid, and with that, the children started salivating.

"Gretel, are you thinking what I'm thinking?"

"That our old man isn't such an idiot after all?" asked Gretel.

Hansel looked over at his father and shook his head. "No. He's still an idiot. But even idiots can have good ideas once in a while. Whaddaya say? You wanna do it?"

"Don't you have to go to school for this? How are we gonna afford it?"

"I'll cosign on a loan," said the father. "We'll get you your schooling."

"Really?" asked Gretel.

"If it gets you out of my house, anything."

So they came up with a plan. First, Gretel had to get her regular driver's license. Neither of the kids owned a car, and only Hansel had his license. Any time either one of them needed to go somewhere, Hansel would drive them in their dad's old turd-on-wheels. If Hansel didn't feel like going anywhere and Gretel needed to get somewhere, her reluctant father would usually end up taking her. They were spoiled brats, it's true; but they would be spoiled brats no longer.

2. Celebrate Good Times

And so it happened. Hansel and Gretel both passed their classes with flying colors, and got their CDL licenses. Gretel first passed her driver's test for her class C license, which she did, also with flying colors, to which she chided Hansel ceaselessly for a while. It took him nine tries to get his. On his first try, he blew parallel parking. Mostly because he didn't know what it was. He thought when you pulled directly into a parking space, that *that* was parallel parking, since you were parallel to the other cars around you. Big fail. The second time, he blew through stop sign after stop sign, since he was quite busy fiddling with the radio. The third time he hit a turtle. The fourth time the turtle hit him. The fifth time the instructor, Mr. Pepin, thought it would be comical to suggest he turn the wrong way up a one way street. Dick. The sixth time, he drove the instructor's car off a bridge and left him there to die. The seventh time, he drove another car off the same bridge, in hopes of searching for the instructor's lost body. The eighth time he didn't have his hands on ten and two. Finally, the ninth time, he decided to get into a different line than he had the last eight tries at the DMV, one that was filled with eighty-eight-year-old ladies. All he had to do this time was fill in his name and flunk an eye exam, and they handed him his license. If only he had known this little trick from day one, he would have been able to save the lives of a couple turtles as well as his driving instructor. Live and learn.

On graduation day, Hansel and Gretel decided to celebrate. They met up with some friends at the local pub to trade war stories and get extremely drunk.

"Long haul trucking?" Chlodwig asked. "Bad idea, man."

"What are you talking about?" Hansel asked. "It's easy money."

"Maybe so," said Chlodwig, "but it's dangerous work."

"Ya," said Hildi. "Dangerous."

"Nah," said Hansel. "I know why you say that, but that was a long time ago. My days of driving off of bridges and whacking into turtles are over. I'm actually a very good driver. And Gretel, here?" He nudged his drunken sister, "she's even better than I am. We're a team."

"It's not about the turtles or peoples you killed," said Chlodwig.

"Ya," said Hildi. "Not about that."

"Then what? What is so dangerous about long haul trucking?"

"There's been a rash of disappearances lately," Chlodwig said.

"Ya," said Hildi. "Poof."

"Cortisone, probably," said Hansel.

"Huh?" Chlodwig asked. "No, not a disappearing rash. A rash of disappearances. Hordes of truckers delivering loads of cookies cross country, never to return."

"Ya," said Hildi. Everyone paused, waiting for her next word. That *ya* just hung in the air like a balloon filled with helium and bumblebees. "Whoreds."

"Nein," said Chlodwig. "Not *whoreds,* hordes."

"Nonsense," said Hansel.

"Numsense," mumbled Gretel.

"Shhh, go back to sleep, sister."

"Hordes!" yelled Gretel.

"Hordes," echoed Hildi.

"Hordes," nodded Chlodwig.

"Hordes, hordes, hordes," the three of them chanted together, which got the whole bar shouting along with them. "Hordes! Hordes! Hordes!" the drunken patrons shouted.

"I don't think *hordes* is the right term to be using," said Hansel. "There are no hordes of truckers, as far as I know. And anyway, we'll be fine. We watch out for each other."

"Oh, like that night back in April? You weren't watching out for her then."

"That was one time. And you're the one who got her drunk and took advantage of her."

"This is true," said Chlodwig, "but still, you should have never let her play the checkers with me when she's drunk. You know I'm a professional."

"Anyway, I can't stay and chitterchat all day," said Hansel. "Come on, Gretel, you ready?"

"One more drinnnk," she said.

"No, I think you're all set."

"One more pleeease."

"They're all out. See?" He turned her head toward the bartender, who just shrugged. "Let's go. I'm sure Dad has some Black Velvet hidden somewhere."

3. Tom Waits

It wasn't long before Hansel and Gretel were able to buy a tractor-trailer of their very own. Their father was able to cosign on that. Even though the old whittler didn't have a cent to his name, he did own his own house, which he put up as collateral. He was glad to do it for his children. This would finally get them out of the house, if even temporarily, till they were able to afford one of their own. They would be on the road most of the time, and that suited the old man just fine. He had just a few words of encouragement: "Don't fuck this up."

And they wouldn't. For the first time in their lives, they were excited about something. For the first time in their lives, they had something productive to do, rather than hang out at home watching TV and playing video games or going out to the bars. They were going to make actual *money*. This was the first job either one of them had (well, except for the paper route that Hansel had picked up when he was twelve, but he could never seem to collect from his customers, so he ended up paying out of his own pocket every time he went back to the office. So you couldn't consider that a job; not really). They had talked to other truckers to get their perspective of life on the open road. Not one of them hated the job itself. They all enjoyed the freedom, and it sure was a kick to get paychecks for doing something that they loved. There were those who were a little melancholy, those who had families back home, but they spent time with what they called "lot lizards", whatever *they* were, to keep their minds off of how much they missed their wives and children.

There were also those who had an irrational fear of disappearing on the job. They told stories of friends they had, that had trucked cookies for a living, leaving for a haul and never coming back. Something about these stories sounded familiar to Hansel and Gretel, then they remembered their friends Chlodwig and Hildi telling them these same stories.

"Relax, they're just stories," Hansel said to his sister, who didn't really seem all that convinced. "Remember Large Marge from *Pee Wee's Big Adventure*?"

"Yeah. Creeped me out. Fucking Tim Burton."

"And that's just one example. The same story's been told over and over. The song "Big Joe and Phantom 309?"

She shrugged.

"By Red Sovine? Made even better by Tom Waits, in my opinion."

"You know I can't stand Tom Waits. His voice drives me up a wall."

"I can't even talk to you right now. Come on, let's listen to some. You may like his older stuff, before his voice became the raspy awesomeness it is today."

"Why must we always have this conversation?" asked Gretel.

"Because. People who don't like Tom Waits just haven't given him enough of a chance."

"You play him all the time."

"Well, get used to it. There'll be a lot of listening to my iPod in the truck."

"As long as we can mix in some Taylor Swift," she said.

"Taylor Swift?"

"What's wrong with Taylor Swift?" she asked.

"Grow up. Anyway, the point I was making was that there are all sorts of stories of the road, most of them are tall tales. About phantom truckers and such."

"Yeah," she said, "but in all those stories, the truckers are the scary part. I've never heard a story where the trucker was the one in danger."

"Well, I have, and I assure you, the cookie story is as old as the trucking industry itself. Or as old as cookies. Whichever came first."

"Really?"

"Sure." In truth, he had never heard any cookie stories before, but he needed to get her out of this fear mindset, before she became too scared and ruined their plans for a bright future.

Their enthusiasm was only slightly derailed the following day when they realized that they got passed over for a spot on *Cargo Wars*. Once again, Hansel had to calm Gretel down.

"But I wanted to be on TV," she said, with all the sadness of a teddy bear left out in the rain.

"I know. I did, too. But we didn't do this to get on TV. We did this to make a life for ourselves. Besides, the cameras would just be a distraction anyway. We need to concentrate on the paycheck, not the fame. Maybe some day we'll get our TV spot, but we just started. Now, quit your crying, and let's see what we can line up for a gig, all right?"

"Okay," she said, still disappointed, but also excited, which left her looking a bit like a drowned rabbit.

They logged into the uShip site for the first time, after one unsuccessful attempt of typing it into Google and inadvertently clicking on a site dedicated to scatological endeavors. To tell the God's honest truth, they did linger on that accidental site a little too long because, let's face it, that shit is interesting. Pun may or may not be intended, depending on your taste in jokes.

"All right, let's see here. BECOME A CARRIER. Yes. ENTER EMAIL. All right."

After checking their email confirmation and setting up their account, they perused some jobs. The listings weren't quite as intriguing as what they showed on the TV show, which made them suspicious that reality TV may not exactly reflect reality. This was a shock to Hansel, and caused a slight ripple in the fabric of his own weltanschauung. He felt like he needed to lie down for a brief second, but it quickly passed, and he proceeded with browsing. He had really had his heart set on a truckload of dwarfs, but the open jobs were far less lucrative at the moment. Pallet of chicken wings to Buffalo, half a truckload of tennis balls to the Pringles factory (finally!), whole truckload of compassion, ethics, and common sense to Washington, D.C. Blah blah blah.

"Ooh, here's one!" Hansel said. "Truckload of cookies to Twig City, California. Says here it's somewhere in the Redwood Forest. That sounds like a blast. I've always wanted to see the great redwoods, haven't you? Gretel? Gretel?"

Her gaze was frozen in horror. "No! No!"

"What's wrong?" Hansel asked.

"We'll never be heard from again!"

"What? Why, because of the cookies? Don't be dumb, Gretel. I told you those are just stories."

"No way am I delivering any cookies to any creepy forest," she said. "Have I mentioned we'll never be heard from again?"

"Sister, think. You've been to the grocery store, right?"

She nodded.

"And you've seen how many cookies are in the cookie aisle, right?"

She nodded.

"If truck drivers were disappearing every time they delivered cookies, do you think there'd be any cookies left in the stores? There'd be no one left to deliver them."

She thought about it. It made a certain kind of sense. Still, she didn't like it. "Can we do something else?" she asked.

"No. My mind's made up. We've come this far. We went through driving school. We got our licenses. This is good money. We're doing this. You need to get over your fears. I'm bidding." He put in a bid for twenty thousand. The next bid came in twenty-three hundred. That was a sobering visit from reality; they would be making much less than twenty thousand dollars.

An hour of bidding, and Hansel put in his final bid for twelve seventy-five. "This is it. This is as low as I'm willing to go." The clock was running down. Only three minutes left. He braced himself on the desk chair. This was very nerve wracking. Hansel had bid on Ebay before, but it was nothing like this. This was like putting all your chips down on roulette and watching the wheel spin. The final seconds ticked away and the clock ran out; it was over. They won the bid.

"Woohoo!" he said, and jumped up out of his chair. He bounced up and down and wiggled his arms like a junkie in a talent show.

"What the hell are you so excited for?" Gretel asked. "We're gonna die!"

"Ah, get over yourself," said Hansel. "We'll be fine."

Gretel sat in the desk chair, scrolling through the job details. "Jesus."

"What's the matter now?"

"Did you even read the job details before you bid?"

"No. Who reads that stuff?"

"Probably everybody else. Look at the address of our pick up."

"Thirty-two Mulligan Street. So?"

"So?" she said. "Have you ever *been* to Mulligan Street?"

"Hell no. Why would I go there? Nothing there but a bunch of Satan worshipers and homeless people."

"Exactly. And look at what time we need to be there. Two a.m. You ever been to Mulligan Street at two a.m.?"

"What did I just say?"

"You just said you never went there. You didn't say what *time* you never went there."

Hansel sighed.

"Do you know how many murders have been committed on Mulligan Street in the past year alone, never mind the surrounding areas?"

"Still with the questions," he mumbled.

He turned to realize she was about two inches from his face. "Yeuh," he said, startled.

"*Do you?*"

"Can't say I do."

"Guess."

"I don't wanna."

"Come on, just guess. How many murders have been committed on Mulligan Street in this past year."

"I don't know," he answered. "Numerous?"

She nodded enthusiastically. "That's correct. Numerous. Numerous murders, Hansel. And we have to go there at two in the morning."

"For the love of the mighty Lord's underpants, Gretel, simmer. We'll be fine. It's a fun job. We'll have a blast, trust me. It's getting late. Get some rest, and I'll see you in the morning. Bright and early."

They awoke at forty-five minutes past midnight, and by 1:30 they were all dressed and ready to hit the road.

"Where you going?" Hansel asked.

"I wanna say bye to Mum and Dad," answered Gretel.

She entered her parents' room, Hansel following closely behind. She approached their bed, and gave her mother a kiss on the cheek. "Bye, Mum. We're off to our first job. I'll make sure to call you."

"Okay, sweetie. Good luck."

"Where's Dad?" she asked.

Their mother felt the other side of her bed. "What time is it?" she asked.

"Half past one."

"Ugh. That's what I feared."

"What?" asked Hansel.

"I don't know if I should be telling you this. You know your father has always been a proud man. Shortly after you two went to bed, he started crying, worrying whether or not he was too harsh on you two. Fearing he did the wrong thing by making you get jobs. I think he's getting empty nest syndrome before you've even left. He went to the pub. This was hours ago."

"He must be drunk as a skunk," Gretel said.

"Must be," Mum agreed. "Whatever. Let him have his space. When your children finally leave home, it's a grieving process. He's trying to adapt in his own way. He'll be fine. He'll be hungover, but he'll be fine."

"All right," Hansel said. "Well, we gotta go. Love you, Mum." He gave his mother a kiss, and added: "You two did the right thing, you know. It was time we grew up."

"I'm glad you feel that way," she said. "Love you both. Be careful."

"We will," Hansel said. "Bye, Mum."

"Bye, Mum," Gretel said.

Hansel pulled into the parking lot of the cookie factory at two a.m. on the dot to the sound of ear-piercing shrieks resembling the mating calls of the undead coming from inside the building. He glanced over at Gretel who, up till this point, was sound asleep, but was now sitting bolt upright in terror. He put on his best fake smile which came off looking like the smirk of a worm drying in the sun after a heavy rainfall. With as much enthusiasm as he could muster, which wasn't very much at all, he said, "We're here."

4. Just Cookies

He backed the rig up to the building like a champ, if the contest was who can suck at backing up the most. Back and forth, back and forth, turning the wheel this way, then that way, then back to this way. For half an hour he tried to get his trailer lined up with the loading dock door. "Dammit!" he said each time he failed to do so.

Gretel opened the passenger side door.

"What are you doing?" asked Hansel.

"Let me try," she said.

Hansel laughed. "You gotta be kidding me."

"What?" she asked.

"I don't mean any offense by this, so please don't take this the wrong way. But you're a girl. I know you passed the course and got your license and everything, but backing up to a dock properly takes vast skills in geometrics and a keen spatial perception, which, as has been proved by science, men are much better at."

She reached over and pinched the skin on his tricep; a move which got him every time.

"Ow, shit!" he exclaimed. "All right, if you insist."

She got in the driver's seat, threw it into reverse, and backed up perfectly with the door, shooting her brother a *don't ever question the abilities of a female if you know what's good for you* look.

He shrugged. "Yeah, but I lined it up for you."

Hansel walked up to the door and rang the bell. Gretel chose to stay in the truck.

The door opened and Hansel was blessed with the sight of a hairy, shirtless man chewing something and digging distractedly in his navel. He looked at his watch, which was the only thing adorning his upper half, and shook his head. "Yer late." He said.

"Sorry, it's my first time backing up to this dock."

"All docks are the same," he said matter-of-factly.

"Well, not really," said Hansel. "See, there's the elevation of the dock itself, the evenness of the ground, the size of the parking lot, the angle of the..."

"Shipping hours are from two to two fifteen."

"That really doesn't give much time to..."

"Yer late," the man repeated. He took another bite of what he had been chewing. It resembled a cookie, but the bite he took caused a thick red fluid to drip out of his mouth and down his chin. Was that blood? The fluid continued to drip down his face the more he chewed, and made a puddle on the floor. Hansel observed the floor was covered in this liquid. A Mexican came by with a floor squeegee, cleaning the floor, pushing the liquid this way and that.

"Um, er, yes, well, if you could just load me up, I'll be on my way."

"Can't," the man said, wiping his chin.

"Why not?" Hansel said, looking away in disgust.

"Shipping hours are from two to..."

"Two fifteen." Hansel finished.

"Right," the man said.

"Look, we really need to be on the road. Is there anything..."

"Fitty bucks."

"Wha?"

"Fitty bucks and I'll load you up."

Hansel did some quick calculating. If he gave the man fifty bucks, they would be short by fifty bucks, if his math was right. That ate into their bottom line. But he'd watched enough of that show to know that things always came up that chiseled away a little at the profit. This was still a well-paying job, and fifty dollars didn't really mean much in the grand scheme of things.

A blood-curdling scream much like the one they heard from outside came from the warehouse.

"Come back here you little shit!" a man's voice said.

"No, no, p-p-please! I'll do anything you say! I'll..."

A loud chopping sound, and the voice was cut short.

"What was that?" Hansel asked.

"That was production," he said. "Always so fuckin' loud, a guy can't think around here. Do you want me to load you up or not?

"Uh... sure. Yeah. Fifty bucks sounds good. Please hurry."

The man got on the forklift and disappeared into another section of the warehouse. He came back with a sad looking pallet of boxes, a few were soaked all the way through, dripping that red fluid onto the floor. A couple of the boxes twitched and jerked. One fell to the floor, hopping and rolling around. The man rolled his eyes and dismounted the forklift in a huff. He waked over to the box and kicked it repeatedly until it stopped moving. He picked it up, the box dripping from the corner, and threw it back on the pallet, which caused a few of the other boxes to shake even more violently. The man looked at Hansel. "Still fresh," he said.

"Still...fresh?" Hansel asked.

"Don't worry. They'll be fine by the time you git to where you're goin'."

"Okay, well, I'm going to go wait in the truck. Here's your fifty bucks."

He tucked two twenties and a ten into the man's cavernous belly button, and had one foot out the door when the man yelled: "Wait!"

"What?!?!?!" Hansel unintentionally shouted back.

The man grabbed his clipboard and held it out to Hansel. He touched the line at the bottom where it said *Driver*, leaving a bloody smear by the X. "Sign here."

"I don't have a pen," Hansel said.

"Friggin' truck driver don't have a pen," the man muttered. He jammed two fingers into his navel, rooted around in there for a bit, pulled out a pen, and handed it over.

Hansel held it with his thumb and forefinger the way you hold a dirty diaper, blew on it, relieving the writing instrument of half of the belly hair surrounding it, and signed his name. As he did so, a squeal came from one of the boxes.

"Shut...the...fuck...up!" the man said, as he kicked a box over and over.

Hansel bolted out the door and ran back into the cab.

"Everything all right?" asked Gretel when she noticed how vexed Hansel appeared.

"Absolutely. Nothing wrong here," Hansel said, forcing a smile. "Just cookies."

5. The Truth About Dad

"What's that?" Gretel asked when she heard the banging coming from the trailer.

"Nothing," Hansel replied. "Trailer's just a little noisy, is all. It's what we get for buying it used. I'm sure we'll get used to it."

Muffled shouts rose up from the trailer. It sounded like someone was yelling *Let us out*.

"I suppose we'll get used to that, too?"

"Used to what?" Hansel said. "I didn't hear anything. I most certainly didn't hear any shouting, if that's what you're asking."

"Hansel? I'm going to ask one question, and you have to answer me truthfully."

"Okay."

"Will you answer me truthfully?"

"Yes, I will answer you truthfully."

"Do you think the cookies are alive?"

Hansel stared straight ahead, his focus on the road.

"Answer the question, Hansel."

"I did. You asked will I answer you truthfully, and I said yes. That was your one shot at a question."

"Okay, can I ask you another question?"

"You just did."

"Okay, can I ask you two more questions that you will answer truthfully to?"

"Yes."

"Do you think the cookies are alive?"

"What? Preposterous. I can assure you the cookies are most certainly dead. Um, I mean, inanimate. Insentient. Most definitely they are just cookies. Not people, if that's what you're asking."

"Hansel?"

"Yeah?"

"Are you scared?"

"Of cookies? Ridiculous."

"Well, I am a little scared myself. I mean, after all those stories of cookie haulers disappearing. And then I wondered why is it that they don't just ship the cookies with a national carrier? Why did they spent a lot more money to have them shipped privately? And now, I hear screaming coming from the back. Don't you find this all a little more than coincidental?"

"I'm tired," Hansel said, avoiding the questions. "Let's go home and get some more shuteye and we'll head out in a few hours."

"I couldn't agree more," said Gretel.

Hansel pulled the rig up in front of their house. They got out, and he searched his pockets for his house key.

"Oh, come on already," Hansel said.

"What?"

"You wouldn't happen to have your house key on you, would you?"

"I left it on the table when we left this morning. Figured Mum and Dad may need a spare. Especially since I assumed you had yours."

"Okie dokie. Hmm." He ventured over to the side of the house and to a window. Thankfully, it was unlocked. They both climbed through, just like they did when they were kids and were sneaking back in after sneaking out to go to an R-rated movie.

"John?" their mother's voice came from her bedroom. "John, is that you? I told you never to come back."

"It's us, Mum," Hansel said, as the living room light flicked on.

"Oh! What are you doing back so early?"

"We have thousands of miles to travel. We need some more sleep before we start our journey. And maybe some breakfast."

"Oh, well, by all means, you know where your beds are. Get some rest, and I'll make you some eggs in a few hours."

"Cool," said Hansel. They went to their respective rooms and tried falling asleep, but all Hansel could think about were the cookies, and how something just didn't seem right about them. All Gretel could think about were the cookies, and also what their mother said when she thought it was their father shuffling in through the window. Needless to say, they would have both been better off if they'd just stayed awake, rather than spend a couple hours tossing and turning and willing sleep that never arrived.

All were seated at the breakfast table when Gretel asked the question. "Mum, what did you mean when you said you told Dad to never come back?"

She sighed, and muttered, "Here goes."

"Oh boy," said Gretel.

"Your father, God bless him, when he had the big talk with you, he made it seem like it was his idea to get you two out of the house, and that you needed to grow up and get jobs."

"It wasn't?" asked Gretel.

"Not exactly. I mean, you two needed to get out and get jobs, for sure. But that wasn't the whole reason. See, your father and I loathe each other. Always have."

"What?" asked Gretel.

"I'm afraid so. But we stuck together and put our happy faces on for your sake. We thought we'd be all done with each other once you two graduated high school. But then you stuck around way too long. And with each passing minute we grew to hate each other more and more. And it's not that your father's a bad person, or that I'm a bad person. We just can't stand the sight of each other any longer. And personally, I can't stand being broke because he won't get himself a real job. He. Just. Keeps. Whittling. It's not enough to keep me happy any longer. It never was, actually. So last night, he went and got himself a hotel room, and vowed never to return. And when I heard you two coming through the window and I thought it was him, I was more than a little disappointed."

"Wow," said Hansel, "you two wasted no time, did you?"

"We did. We wasted years together. We couldn't be in the same room with each other for one more minute."

The kids looked disappointed. Especially Gretel, who had a tear in her eye.

"I'm sorry you had to find out like this. I was planning on telling you once you were both on your feet and happy."

Hansel put a hand on his mother's shoulder. "It's okay, Mum. I get it."

"You do?"

"Yes. I mean, I love the man to pieces, but he was kind of a loser."

"Hansel!" his mother scolded, but couldn't suppress a little laugh. "Oh, my. Look at the time. I assume you two have had a good breakfast?"

"Yes," both said. "It was delicious."

"Okay, good. Now get out."

"Mum!" Gretel said.

"Sorry," their mother said, "but I have a gentleman caller coming soon, and I need to get ready."

"Jesus," said Gretel. "You couldn't wait till Dad was gone a full day?"

"Your mother hasn't been laid in years," she said. "And I'm certainly not getting any younger. Now, go on. Beat it."

They put their shoes on and walked outside.

"What on Earth is that God-awful racket?" Mum asked when she heard the sounds coming from the truck.

"Trailer's old," Hansel said. "Come on, Gretel. Let's let Mum get her freak on."

Gretel shuddered. "Gross," she said.

6. The Irving Station

Twelve hours heading west on I-80. Of course, to a veteran truckist, twelve hours is a walk in the park. But to these two crazy kids who had, let's face it, spent the last twenty-something years of their lives doing nothing, it was a challenge. Sure, they had spent most of that time doing nothing on their asses, but sitting on your ass for twelve hours in a truck, actually having to pay attention to things, I mean, wow, dude. That took a lot out of someone.

Hansel had insisted on driving the first leg of the journey, and he was looking forward to Gretel taking the wheel after they had gotten some rest. They had gotten a much later start than they anticipated, but sharing a last breakfast with their mum was worth it. They had plenty of time to make it to the west coast; they may as well take their time getting there. He was lousy with directions, always had been. Luckily, however, their truck was installed with the Breadcrumbs Satellite Navigation System. They had never heard of this particular brand of navigator before, and other truckers said it was the bottom of the barrel. Maybe with the money they made from this job, they would get a better system; you know, putting money back into the business and all that. But right now, they would have to make do with what they had. I mean, how bad could it be, right?

Hansel pulled into the Skeeter Haven Motel ("A trucker's paradise. Lot lizards welcome") at eight in the evening. Across the way was an Irving gas station that looked like it also contained a small restaurant inside.

"Lot lizards?" Gretel asked. "What the hell are lot lizards?"

"They're just what they sound like," Hansel said.

"Why would they welcome lizards into the motel?"

"Another way to make money," Hansel said.

"What's with the sign on the door?" she asked. "Lizards can't read."

"You're right," he agreed. "Most of them can't."

"Are they slimy or scaly?"

"They come in all varieties," Hansel said. "Some of them are both slimy *and* scaly."

"I guess I'm not sure how they make money off of lizards."

"It's not the lizards that pay," Hansel explained. "It's the truckers that get blowjobs from them, or what-have-you. Sometimes they want to do things to the lizards that their wives won't do for them at home, like have anal sex with them."

Her mouth acquired that squiggly look that Charlie Brown gets when he's confused.

"You go get us a table at the Irving. I hear they have good pie." Hansel said to his sister. "I'll check us in."

"Okay, be careful of the lizards."

"Don't worry," said Hansel. "I wouldn't touch them with a wet blanket if they were on fire. You be careful of the lizards, too. They'll probably be in the restaurant chowing down waiting for the truckers to arrive."

"They serve lizards in there?"

"No. They serve meatloaf and pie."

"Haha. I mean they serve food *to* the lizards?"

"IRVING DOES NOT DISCRIMINATE!" Hansel shouted.

"All right, all right!" she yelled back. "Calm down. I'll get us a table."

She entered the Irving, walked past the cash registers, and into the restaurant. A sign by the cashier said "SEAT YOURSELF DAMMIT", which she thought was a little demanding, but whatever.

The dining room was full. This was strange; not because it was such a late hour, but because the parking lot of both the Irving and the motel were fairly empty. Where did all these people come from? She didn't see any lizards, but there sure were a lot of weird-looking folks, who had a major staring problem. She didn't really like being stared at, and she could feel the blood of embarrassment flooding her cheeks.

"Um, Large Marge sent me?" she said.

"Ahh, shuddup and siddown and have some pie," a patron said from the corner of the room, and a glob of whipped cream went flying, almost hitting her.

Gretel was appalled. She was beginning to doubt the tastiness of their desserts. Any pie that wasn't worthy of standing on its own and felt it had to hide under whipped cream was not a pie she felt she should give credence to. She wasn't a big fan of pies, anyway. But she *was* hungry, and meatloaf and mashed potatoes sounded awesome.

The waitress came over. "What can I getcha?"

"I'm gonna wait for my brother before I order. Can I just get a beer to start?"

"We don't serve no alcohol here," the waitress said.

"Can I go into the store section and buy a beer?"

"Sure, but you can't drink it here. We ain't got no liquor license."

"Liquor?" Gretel said. "No, no, I just want a beer. No liquor."

The waitress walked away to another table without saying one more word to Gretel.

"Hey beautiful," a male voice said from over her shoulder. She turned around to see an odd little man with a quirky left eye and beard stubble that reached far below his neck.

"Hey."

"What's a guy like me doing in a girl like you?"

She put her palm to her face. "Has that line ever worked?"

"Dunno," the man said. "We'll find out tonight."

She removed the palm from her face and applied it to his cheek, hard.

"Ow!" the man said. "The fuck?"

"I'm waiting for my husband," she said. "Get lost."

He bowed like a court jester in front of an audience of fried oysters. "My sincerest apologies, young lady. I had no idea. I was under the false assumption you were a lizard."

"Do I look like a lizard?" she asked.

"Frankly, no. You are much better looking than any lizard I've come across."

"Gee, thanks."

"And I've come across a lot, if you get my drift," he said, as he mimed masturbating.

"Gross."

"Again, my apologies. It's just I've been rejected by every other woman in this restaurant. Making the rounds, you know."

She looked around and observed that every other woman in the diner was toothless and covered in scabs which they were scratching with much gusto. "And you thought I'd say yes?"

"Not necessarily."

Come on, Hansel, hurry up, she thought.

"So what are you doing here, anyway? On vacation?"

"Making a delivery," she said.

"You're a *truck driver?*" he asked. "No way."

"Yes. I am a truck driver. What? Women can't drive trucks?"

"Oh, no. They can. It's just, every woman truck driver I've seen looks, well, only slightly better than those ladies over there." He gestured to a table with four babbling, itching women, three of them letting their scabs fall to the floor, and the fourth eating hers. "You are much too good looking to be driving trucks. You should be a model or something."

"Gee. Thanks."

Hansel, what the fuck is taking you so long?

"Where ya headed?"

"California."

"Oh, really? Where at?"

"Twig City."

"Hmm. Never heard of it. And I've been just about everywhere in that state. Sounds made up."

"Well, it's not. Check the map."

She was being facetious, but he pulled out his phone anyway, Googling it.

"Nope. Not on here. See? Told ya."

"Well, we found it on our GPS, so it obviously exists."

"Hmm. What you got for a GPS?"

"I forget the name of it. Bread-something."

"*Breadcrumbs?*" He laughed. "Oh, man. That's the worst navigation system ever. Half the towns that should be on there aren't, and the rest of it is filled with fictitious locations."

"Don't they all use the same satellies?" she asked.

"Most do. Not Breadcrumbs, though. They have been around longer than any of the other big names. Most of the great ones learned from Breadcrumbs' mistakes. I hear their satellite is nothing but an old popsicle stick that someone hot glued a couple mirrors onto."

"Whatever. It knows how to get to Twig City, and that's all that matters."

"Whatcha haulin'?" he asked.

Jesus Christ, give it a rest, guy.

"Cookies," she answered.

His eyes widened, and he backed away, slowly, stumbling over chairs and making a crucifix with his fingers. "El Diablo!" he screamed, and ran full speed into the front window, shattering the glass. He sprinted to his truck, started the engine, and took off, honking.

What the fuck was that about? She thought.

"You ready to order or what?" the waitress asked, unfazed.

"Still waiting for someone, thanks."

The waitress stormed off in a huff.

At long last, Hansel walked in, and grabbed a seat at Gretel's table. "You order yet?"

"I was waiting for you. What took you so long?"

"I was all set to check in, when the owner happened to ask what I was hauling. I told him, and he freaked out and threw himself out the window."

"Strange," she said.

"Sure is. What happened here?"

"Same thing. I told some guy what we were carrying, and he called me El Diablo and threw himself out a window."

"Hm. The people in this town."

"Yeah," Gretel agreed. "Weirdos."

THE ALPHABET BOOKS: ABC

"*Now* are you ready to order?" the waitress asked.

"Lost my appetite," Gretel said. "You?" she asked Hansel.

"I'm good," he said.

"Oh for fuck sake," said the waitress. "At the very least, have some pie."

"Ehh," said Gretel, "not a big pie fan."

"Not a big pie fan?" said the waitress, "NOT A BIG PIE FAN???"

"Yeah, not really."

"What do you have against pie?"

"Not big into fruit or pudding, and it seems like that's all pie ever is. Fruit or pudding."

"Oh, honey. You ain't never had a pie like an Irving pie. Look over there at our wall of pies."

She looked over. There were a lot of pies.

"We have more than just fruit and pudding pies. We have chicken pie, turkey pie, veal pie, peanut butter inside out pie, Tollhouse cookie pie, I mean, the options are endless."

"Ooh, Tollhouse cookie pie. I'll have that," she said.

"Very good," said the waitress. "And for you, sir?"

"Do you have apple?"

"No."

"No apple?"

"What did I just say?"

"Who doesn't have apple?"

"*We* don't have apple."

"Like, you never have apple, or you're just out at the moment?"

"Like, we never have apple."

"But apple really is the *only* pie, you know,"

"Don't be a pussy."

"The upside down peanut butter one, then."

"*Inside out!*" she said, clearly irritated. "Great choice." She skipped away gaily like she was Shirley Temple. Not Shirley Temple in her heyday, but an old Shirley Temple with a daughter who played bass for the Melvins in the '80s.

The waitress came back seconds later with two slices of pie.

"Oh boy, this sure looks good," Hansel said. He dug the three tines of his old-fashioned fork into his peanut butter pie, and took a bite. "Mmm. Tastes good, too. Try yours."

She looked down at the piece of pie on her own plate. It was the *shape* of a wedge of pie. That's where the comparison ended. The steam rising up from the hot dessert carried with it a stench the likes of which none of you fine people will ever have the misfortune of sniffing. And if you do, may God have mercy on your soul. She dug her fork in, which for some odd reason only had two tines, which made her a little jealous of her brother. Not only did he get what appeared to be the better dessert, he also got the better fork. A squealy, squeaky sound issued forth from the pie as the fork penetrated it. A gunky, snotty sludge the color of used motor oil and old mayonnaise dripped down from where the tines pierced, and blood ran out of the pores where the chocolate chips rested like blackheads on an old man's back. She risked taking a bite, and it tasted like pig meat wrapped in a 100 percent cotton undershirt.

"Excuse me," she called to the waitress, whose name was probably Darlene. "Something's wrong with my pie."

She waddled on over at a leisurely pace and examined Gretel's dessert plate. Her nametag did, in fact, say Darlene. "What's the matter, sweetie? Looks fine to me."

"You don't think it looks kinda sketchy?" Gretel asked.

"Well," she whispered, "to tell you the truth, it's not as good as it used to be. We switched vendors."

"*Switched vendors? Switched vendors???*"

"Yeah. Cutting corners. Saving some bucks."

"*Saving some bucks???*"

"Shaving some ducks," the waitress answered.

"How many pieces of pie have you sold since you switched vendors, ducks notwithstanding?"

"Quite a few," said the waitress. "You know, come to think of it, nobody ever orders a second one."

"Because they probably drop dead after they leave. Anyway, can we have the check?"

"Do you want anything else?"

"No. That's why I asked for the check."

"Can I bring you a box to put the pie in?"

She thought for a second. "Sure. What the hell. May get hungry later watching Jimmy Kimmel."

7. cookies

"Sister. Wake up!"

"Huh? What time is it?"

"Three in the morning. You gotta come see this."

She got out of bed, slowly. "Three in the morning? This better be good."

"Hurry up!"

"All right. Let me get my clothes on. Jeez."

"No time. Come on!"

"I'm not going out there in my nightgown. Too many creeps around here."

She put her clothes on, slowly.

"I'll be outside," Hansel said. He grabbed a lamp off the dresser, yanked it out of its socket, and threw it on the bed. "You're gonna need this." He ran out the door.

"It won't work if it's not plugged in," she shouted after him. "Don't you know how lamps work?"

"Just bring it," he shouted over his shoulder as he sprinted off.

Now fully dressed, she grabbed the lamp and headed outside. "Hansel?" she called.

"Over here! By the trailer!"

The parking lot was dimly lit, but it was enough to see that the scene was not good. Hansel was kneeling down on the ground beating the shit out of something with a Gideon's Bible, blood getting all over his face and neck. The back door of the trailer had been busted wide open. The light in back was on, and she could see that half of their load was missing.

"What the...?" Gretel asked.

"Hurry! Get as many cookies as you can! Use the lamp if you have to, and beat the shit out of them, and throw them in the truck. Be careful, though. They bite." He held up his hand so she could see his injury.

"Holy shit."

"Never mind," he said. "Just get them!"

No sooner had he said that than one began climbing her leg. She raised the lamp up and brought it down on the cookie, squashing it even flatter than it was. She thanked God that the lamp was made out of metal, and not porcelain. However, her leg wasn't made of metal, and a pain shot up her shin and into the back of her neck when the second blow hit her leg instead of the cookie. "Motherfuck!" she yelped, as she fell to the ground.

"You all right?" Hansel asked, still beating the same cookie.

"No," she answered, brushing a cookie from her arm and hobbling away.

"Where you going?"

"Back inside. This job isn't worth it!"

"Wait for me!" he called after her, abandoning the cookie and following her.

She approached a room that had its light on and its door open.

"What are you doing?" he asked. "That's not our room."

"Gonna get some help."

"Don't go in there!" Hansel yelled.

"I'm gonna get some..." her words ceased, and a scream erupted from her the likes of which Hansel had never heard before.

"Told you," he muttered, as he followed her into the room.

A man lay face down on the carpeted floor. He appeared to have bites all over him, and chunks were missing from his ass, back, arms, legs, and the back of his neck. A skittering noise came rushing forth, and a cookie shot out from nowhere and sunk its teeth into the man, tearing away another piece of flesh and issuing a tiny birdlike squeak before retreating back underneath the bed. Three more cookies came charging out from the bathroom.

He put a hand on her arm and dragged her out, and all the way back to their own room, locking and chaining the door behind him.

"What the fuck was that?" she asked, hysterical.

"I don't know," he said. "Something's not right with the cookies."

"Something's not right with the cookies? *Something's not right with the cookies??* No shit something's not right with the cookies. I told you. I *told* you, Hansel"

"Told me what?"

"Really??? I told you this was a bad idea. I told you there was truth to those cookie tales all the truckers told."

"Aww, that's probably just a coincidence," said Hansel.

"What are you talking about? Coincidence? That doesn't even make sense." She reached for her phone.

"What are you doing?" he asked.

"It's a lost, *ow!*" she kicked a cookie that bit her toe across the room. She opened the door and booted it outside. "It's a lost cause. Our trailer's destroyed, by now our product is scattered all over town, and the cookies are attacking us. The lady that's expecting delivery left her contact number. I'm calling this off."

He pulled the phone out of her hand. "Now, now, let's not get hasty. Think about this for a minute. It's very early in the morning. Let's give it a few hours before we make that decision."

"It's a couple hours behind in California. Maybe she's still awake."

"Maybe. But it's rude."

"Are you kidding me right now? Rude? *We're being attacked by cookies!*"

"Fine. Do what you gotta do." He handed the phone back to her and tore a sheet from the bed.

"What are *you* doing?" she asked.

"Cookies broke the latch on the trailer door. Gonna tie it closed."

"You're worried about cargo??"

"No. I'm worried about more of them escaping and attacking people. I don't know if our insurance covers this kind of thing."

"All right. Be careful."

He stopped to stomp a cookie into a bloody pulp. "I will," he said.

MARC RICHARD

8. COOKIES!

Those who didn't really know her well called her a witch. Others, well, let's face it. There were no others. There were those who didn't know her well, and those who didn't know her at all. And maybe they were right; maybe she *was* a witch. Hell, she wasn't really sure she knew herself all that well, either. At least, that's what her therapist had said once. Maybe she shouldn't have stopped going to him so suddenly. Maybe she should have had a little mercy on him, and let him alone to do his thing. He really was good at what he did, and she could have benefited from his wisdom if she had continued her sessions. But in reality, she was more excited about baking than she was about becoming a better person. It was her *raison d'être*. It may even be said that baking was a better therapy than sitting and talking about feelings. Her cookies never told her things like she didn't know herself all that well. Okay, a few of them did, but that was the batch she made out of her therapist, so it was to be expected. Anyway, that was quite a long time ago, and those cookies had fully dried and hardened and didn't talk or move anymore. Nor did they bleed. Unlike the cookies that she ordered from the factory.

Anyway, she may or may not have been a witch, depending on your definition of that word. She certainly *looked* like a witch. Always had. Maybe that's why she had been shunned by society, and why she shunned society back. She was an ugly baby. So ugly, in fact, that her parents had abandoned her, strictly because of her looks. But don't judge; you would have done the same. She was left at an orphanage, and there she grew up. The older she got, the uglier she got. She didn't make one friend in the orphanage. Not one. There was one person who took pity on her, and that was the cook, Annette. A beautiful, middle-aged woman who really had no business talking to someone as hideous as her, but she had a heart of gold. One day, she had been crying alone in her room when there was a knock on the door. It was Annette. She asked her if she would like to come help her in the kitchen. And that's where her love of cooking began. She especially fell in love with baking. She had a huge sweet tooth, and was always first in the dessert line. Now that she knew how to make desserts herself, she started experimenting. She began using ingredients that Annette had never used before, such as apple sauce and peanuts. Annette would take her on trips to the store to get other ingredients that she wanted. She could have anything she desired, as long as she didn't go over budget.

    The other children in the orphanage loved her desserts as well, but this didn't buy her any affection from them. They still stayed away from her and made fun of her both behind her back and to her face. One day, one of the brattier kids had called her a witch. He said she looked just like a witch from the fairy tales. She had always thought so, but didn't realize that others had until this boy said it out loud. This filled her with such rage that she attacked the boy with a knife and cut him up into little pieces. He *was* kinda dumb for making fun of her in a kitchen, where there were so many weapons around. She needed to find a way to get rid of the body, quickly before anyone caught her. Luckily, she had been halfway through making a batch of cookies.

His body had made the dough taste absolutely terrible, so she added more sugar and flour and eggs and chocolate and baking soda and butter until it once again tasted decent. The batch made eight dozen cookies. She supposed that wasn't *too* many. If it was, she'd just freeze what the kids didn't eat.

But there weren't any left to freeze. Every last one had been gobbled up. The house mother had begun chastising them for being such little piggies, but after she had tried a cookie, she kept the piggy comments to herself and ate half a dozen.

So, the cookies were an even bigger hit than the rest of her desserts. So finally, did she earn some respect? No. The teasing continued, and the kids were more merciless than ever. And so, one by one, the orphans disappeared until there were only a few of them left. And one day, the house mother found the witchy girl missing, too. She had to go; they were getting suspicious of foul play. Yes, they probably should have gotten suspicious after the first few had vanished, but nobody really noticed right away, as there were so damned many of them. Anyway, she knew that soon she would be the one they would turn against first with their accusations, so she left. She was thirteen, plenty old enough to be on her own, anyway.

She found a small shack tucked far away in the woods, where she wouldn't be bothered. Loneliness was foreign to her, as she'd really been alone her entire life. She did miss Annette a little, but toward the end even Annette had started acting a little strange toward her. She knew that soon she would have lost her, too. Perhaps some people were just destined to be alone. She made occasional trips into town to rob people's pantries of the basic staples, so that she didn't have to give up the one thing that brought her joy: Baking. After eating cookies made out of human meat for so long, however, these so-called normal cookies just didn't taste as good. It didn't take long for the homeless population to start a steady decline, and it wasn't due to a sudden abundance of available jobs.

Baking was an obsession with her. This transitioned from all baked goods to just cookies. It reached a point where she made a ridiculous amount more than she could ever eat. She had no one to share them with, and even though she had a great metabolism, no one could eat that many cookies and not grow sideways. Her small shack was at the point where it couldn't handle any more cookies; she either needed to find something else to do with them or get a bigger house. Or both. That's it! Both! She knew what to do; she would build additions onto her house with the dried-up cookies that were too stale to eat. Due to the meat and bone meal, they hardened up like bricks, rather than just crumbling. They would make perfect building materials.

The bigger her house became, the bigger she wanted it. Soon, it wasn't a problem of too many cookies, but not enough. Years had gone by, which saw the invention of the Internet. She used this to see where she could buy cookies that were as tough as hers. After sampling several different brands, she finally found one that was satisfactory. Not *great*, and far from edible, and sometimes they came in still twitching (obviously they were using similar recipes), but after drying them out, they made better building blocks than hers. It wasn't too long before she was buying them by the truckload. Since she didn't have many visitors, and she was becoming tired of hunting down the homeless and dragging them back to her house, it just became a convenience to use the truck drivers as ingredients. Every trucker that delivered to her house had a one-way ticket.

Her phone was ringing. Her phone never rang.

9. Birds and Breadcrumbs

"Hello?" came an androgynous voice from the other end of the line.

"Hello, sir or madam?" Gretel greeted/inquired.

"It's madam," the woman answered.

"Nice to meet you. My name is Gretel."

"What do you want?" asked the voice. "I'm very busy here."

Gretel sneaked a peek outside the curtain, where Hansel was attempting to tie the truck's door closed while single-handedly taking on several mutant cookies.

"Same here," Gretel said.

"Yes, well, what can I do for you, Gretchen?"

"Um, Gretel, ma'am."

"Gretchen, Grace, whatever; time's a tickin'."

"Uh, we have a delivery of cookies, um, scheduled to be delivered, um, in a few days."

"Oh, you're the truck driver? Well, why didn't you say so, dear?"

"Um, I just did, so..."

"A female truck driver, hmm? Well, doesn't that just beat all."

"Yes ma'am." A flying cookie hit the window, startling her. "My brother and me."

"Two of you? Well, won't that be a treat? I'm not paying extra for that, you know."

"Why would you pay extra for two of us?"

"No reason," the lady said.

"Anyway, I suppose I should inform you, uh..." she looked out the window again. The trailer door seemed to be tied up tight. All was fairly quiet, until Hansel came barreling across the parking lot at full sprint, followed by an army of cookies. He pounded on the door, and Gretel opened it. Hansel ran inside, leaned against the door, and threw the deadbolt. The rush was unnecessary, as the cookies were still about thirty paces behind, some slinking about like slugs, some tiptoeing on little feet, some rolling along on their edges, but all moving fairly slowly. So, the good news is they could be outrun. This was helpful information.

"Inform me of what?" the lady on the other end asked.

"Um, half or more of your load is missing."

"MISSING???" She screamed. "What do you mean missing?"

"You wouldn't believe it if I told you."

"Try me."

"We woke in the middle of the night to find that they had escaped out of the back of the trailer. They're running amok!"

"And what, you don't have a latch on your trailer?"

"Of course we do, but they broke through!"

"Nonsense. Those latches get tested quite rigorously. You must have purchased a cheap trailer."

"Well, in all honesty, we're just starting out, and couldn't really afford a...wait a minute. Have you heard a word of what I've been saying? The cookies are alive!"

"Missy, I have the right mind to send you back to the factory and pick up the rest of the load. On your dime. Where are you?"

Gretel told her.

"Never mind. There's no time to waste. Just bring me what you have and we'll have to settle what I actually owe you when you get here. I tell you what, girly, it'll be a lot less that what you are charging."

"But the cookies took off by their own volition. We shouldn't be held responsible for that."

"Can you gather the escapees and get them back on the truck?"

"Are you fucking kidding me?" Gretel asked. "They're biting us!"

"Language!" the lady admonished. "Just keep coming my way and I'll see what I can do when you get here. Good bye."

"Okay, well, good bye, then," Gretel said to a dead line.

"What did she say?" Hansel asked his sister.

"She's not too happy about the lost product for sure. I have a feeling we're going to lose money on this job."

"Ya think?"

Gretel's phone buzzed with a text.

"Who's that?" asked Hansel.

"It's that lady. She wants me to send her a picture of us."

"A picture? What for?"

"How the hell should I know?" said Gretel.

"What a weirdo."

"I know. What should we do?"

"Send her one," said Hansel. "Don't see what harm there is in it." He got close to his sister, put his arm around her, and smiled.

Gretel took the selfie and pressed send. "Okay. Are we ready to roll?"

"Now more than ever," Hansel said.

They made their way to the truck, stomping on cookies that were trying to bite their ankles on the way. Hansel double-checked inside the cab to make sure there were no baked goods waiting to attack him, gave Gretel the all-clear signal, and hopped in.

Gretel's phone buzzed again.

"What's it say?" asked Hansel.

"It says: You two look like very sweet ingredients."

"Ingredients? What the hell is that supposed to mean?"

"How should I know? I didn't write it."

Gretel texted back: INGREDIENTS?

The text came back: I MEANT PEOPLE. I'LL NVR GET USED TO THIS AUTO-CORRECT

"She meant people," Gretel said.

"Oh, well that makes more sense," he said. He started the engine and headed toward the freeway while Gretel involved herself with her Angry Birds app.

She spoke without looking up from her phone. "Brother?"

"Yes?"

"Do you think we're making a big mistake?"

"Probably."

A few more minutes went by.

"Brother?"

"Yes?"

"Do you think we should call it quits? I mean, maybe we should just find the nearest landfill, dump our cargo, head home, get our trailer repaired, and move on to the next job."

"You're kidding, right? This is our first job. We'll be getting a rating from this lady on the site. You know how important reviews are? They can make or break a business.

And only having one review, our first one, being a one-star? We'll be lucky if we get approved for any more jobs."

"I have a feeling our review is already going to be pretty low. We lost half her load."

"Let's just see this through. Maybe when we get there we'll find out she's actually reasonable, and we'll be able to work out some sort of deal for a good review. Or at least a non-shitty one."

"I sure hope so. Brother?"

"Yes?"

"Do you think we'll make it out of this alive?"

He thought for a second. "Way I see it, we got a fifty-fifty shot."

"That doesn't sound all that encouraging."

"It's not. But would you rather lose everything that we have invested into this job, lose our potential to get any more jobs, turn around, head home, and have to tell Mum and Dad that we failed?"

"Uh... yes?"

"Fine. I'll drop you off at the next truck stop. You can call Dad and ask him to come pick you up."

"No, forget it. Let's just keep going."

"Thought so."

Trying to keep her mind off things, her attention turned back to her Angry Birds game.

"What the hell?" Hansel said a few minutes later.

"What?"

"Look at the GPS."

She did. Somehow her Angry Birds app had taken over the screen of their Breadcrumbs GPS. "Huh," said Gretel. "That's pretty neat."

"Yeah. Neat. Can you turn the phone off? It's interfering with the system."

"Aw, come on. I need something to keep my mind off stuff."

"Turn it off," he repeated.

"Just one more round?"

"Okay. One more. Then shut it down."

Two seconds went by, and the round was over. She never had been able to make it past the first pipe. She closed out of the app. "Bah, why do I even bother?"

And as the app on her screen shut down, so did the app on the GPS. The system shut off.

"What the?" Hansel said.

The screen turned back on.

"Oh. Okay," Hansel said.

The screen flashed blue, purple, pink, and yellow.

"What the?" Hansel said.

A progress bar appeared at the bottom of the screen. CONFIGURING... it said.

"Oh. Okay," Hansel said.

The screen once more restarted.

"What the?" Hansel said.

The screen came back on with another progress bar. APPLYING UPDATES... it said.

"Oh. Okay," Hansel said.

When the progress bar finally filled to one hundred percent, the GPS did not pop back up. However, Angry Birds did.

"You're kidding me," he said, fuming.

Gretel had a guilty look on her face. "Sorry."

He calmed down a bit before he spoke. "Not your fault. They told us the system was junk."

"It's all right. I have GPS on my phone."

"Twig City doesn't show on any other GPS, remember?"

"Oh yeah."

"I mean, I kinda know where I'm going. We just need to follow this freeway. I'll stop somewhere and get a gazetteer."

"Do they still make those things?" Gretel asked.

"I think so."

After a moment of silence, Gretel began chuckling.

"What's so funny?" Hansel asked.

"Haha. Think about it," said Gretel. "You could say that the birds ate the breadcrumbs, couldn't you?"

"No, Gretel. No, you couldn't."

10. Ranger Rick

As luck would have it, they didn't have to stop for a gazetteer anyway, as after multiple times unplugging and re-plugging, hitting with fists, and pressing the tiny reset button with a straightened paper clip, the Breadcrumbs system finally rebooted and seemed to be working fine. According to the GPS, they had just fourteen hours left till they reached Twig City, California.

The rest of the trip saw no more shenanigans from the trailer. Either the remaining cookies in the back were completely dead, in hibernation, or were never alive in the first place. They drove nonstop until they reached Eureka, when the GPS told them they had arrived at their destination. This was odd, as the sign they just passed clearly told them they were in Eureka, not Twig City.

"What do we do now?" Gretel asked.

"We get out and ask someone," said Hansel.

They did. Nobody had heard of Twig City. Hansel supposed he shouldn't have been shocked, since that's how their luck had been going lately.

But then they made a stop at one particular convenience store, giving it one more go, asking everyone in there. Again, nobody had heard of it. Then they asked the one guy that was left. The one they were scared to approach. The one with the bad comb-over and no upper teeth and his neck stretched out like a giraffe with his arm in a box of Pepperidge Farms. He pulled the imitation Oakleys down below his little nub of a nose, and they noticed that his eyes were completely white. He twitched a couple times and pulled a notepad and pen from his front pocket. He scribbled a little something, tore the paper out of the book, and folded it several times until it wouldn't fold anymore. He placed the scrap in Hansel's hand, and closed it tight with his own. He placed a finger across his lips, shooed them off, and resumed munching his Chessmen.

"Okay, ready?" Hansel asked, and Gretel nodded.

"Want anything? Box of cookies or something?"

She glared. Guess not.

They got back in the truck and Hansel unfolded the note.

"What's it say?" Gretel asked impatiently.

He shook his head and handed her the note. Nothing but a crudely drawn arrow.

"The hell is that supposed to mean?" she asked.

Hansel shrugged.

"Should we go back in and ask him?" she asked.

Hansel shook his head.

"What do we do?" she asked.

Hansel put the note on the dashboard, the arrow pointing straight ahead. "We follow the arrow," he said.

They drove for half an hour or so in a direction that just happened to be north, finally coming upon a sign that said: REDWOOD NATIONAL AND STATE PARKS. WELCOME!

"Do you think it's *in* the park?" Gretel asked.

"Who knows?" said Hansel.

A little further up the road and they reached a quaint little ranger's station with deer grazing out in the field in the back.

"How sweet," Gretel said. "Well, if one person would know, it would be a park ranger."

A kind looking man stepped out of the hut. "Welcome to the Redwood Park," he said.

"Oh, no need," said Hansel. "The sign already did."

"Huh?" he asked.

"Never mind. Bad joke. Listen, you wouldn't know how to get to Twig City, would you, Ranger...?"

"Rick," the ranger said.

"You're kidding," Hansel said.

The ranger looked at him questioningly.

"Ranger Rick?" Hansel asked.

"That's right." He was waiting to have the joke explained to him, but Hansel decided to drop it.

"Anyway," said Hansel, "Twig City. Know how to get there?"

"Never heard of it," the ranger said.

"Of course not," said Gretel. "Come on, Hansel. Let's turn around."

"Afraid I can't let you do that," said the ranger.

"Why not?" asked Gretel.

"Once you drove past the welcome sign you entered Park limits. I'm going to have to ask you to open the back of your truck."

"No!" shouted Hansel.

"Hiding something?" asked the ranger.

"No," said Hansel. "Not exactly. Wh...uh...*why* do you have to search the trailer, exactly?"

"You're in a national park. It's a terrorism thing."

"Oh," said Hansel. "Understandable. However, I would sincerely advise against it, for your own safety."

"Aha!" said the ranger. "So you *are* hauling dangerous materials. What'cha got? Guns? Razors? Whirling tornadoes of knives? Bombs? Drugs? You got drugs, home skillet?"

"What?" asked Hansel. "No. Cookies, man. Just cookies."

The ranger went to the rear of the trailer, and came back with a smile. "Cookies, huh? Well, why didn't you say so. Wait here."

As they were waiting, Gretel turned to Hansel. "I don't like this one bit. What's going on here?"

"I don't know, sister. Just sit tight."

The ranger came back with a park map. Hansel took it and gave it a once-over. There was a red X etched in what looked like the middle of nowhere. Rick suddenly had a very helpful tone. "Okay, so what you're gonna do is follow this road here, take a left here, a right there, where you'll see a chocolate river. Follow the river until you come to a beautiful mansion made out of cookies. You can't miss it."

"Chocolate river?" Gretel asked.

"That's right. Finest one in the state. Now, I'm sorry for giving you a hassle, it's just there have been a lot of folks looking for Twig City through the years, and not all have good intentions. There are lots of folks who want to bring harm to the lady you're making the delivery to. Yes, my job is to protect the park. But I also make sure no one comes looking for the old lady with malicious intent."

"Well, that's very nice of you," said Hansel. "But how do you know we're actually making a delivery, and not hauling truckloads of Samurai swords or something?"

"The state of your trailer. I saw the way you had the back tied, and knew right away. Cookies messed your door up, didn't they?"

"Sure did," said Hansel.

"Yeah. They'll do that."

"Some of them even got away," said Gretel.

"Say what, now?" asked Rick.

"Some of them escaped," she repeated.

Rick buried his face in his hands and shook his head. "Damn," he said. "Old lady's gonna be pissed. You don't want to get on her bad side."

"It's okay," said Gretel. "She knows."

"All right," Rick said, hitting the button that opened the gate. "Best of luck to you. Safe travels."

"Thanks," said Hansel, then: "Hey, Rick?"

"Yeah?"

"Have any truck drivers ever gone through and not come back?"

"Hahaha," said Rick, chewing on a squirming cookie, blood dripping down his chin. "You'll be fine. Take care now."

Hansel started the engine and drove on. He looked at Gretel. "I don't know. I get the feeling something isn't right."

11. The Chocolate River

The road the ranger had mapped out for them was quite possibly one of the most convoluted, twisty ways they could have gone, according to the map itself. The problem was, he explained before they took off, the roads were not built for tractor trailers. Typically any trailers that made deliveries to the parks delivered to the stations along the perimeter. If anything needed to be taken farther in, the loads were then moved onto smaller trucks owned by the park, that then took the merchandise from there. There were several logistical issues with this when it came to cookie delivery, not the least being disappearing park employees. So the old lady had a select few rangers help her map out a route the trucks could take. One where the roads were wide enough. One where there weren't any curves too sharp for a trailer to make the turns. One where you didn't have to drive through the middle of a goddamned tree. Every now and then, on their own time of course, the few rangers who were in the know did maintenance above and beyond what the park did, such as clearing any branches over the road that were lower than fourteen feet.

Why, you ask? Why on earth would anyone help this crazy old lady with her homicidal lifestyle? But you've probably answered your own question. It was the cookies. There was something about the old witch's recipe that gave the cookies powers that were almost magical. Sure, years ago, the old lady started making them out of human bodies as convenience, a way to hide evidence. But the more she did it, the more she noticed that they were having a most profound effect on her. They helped her feel healthy and vibrant and young. She couldn't remember exactly how old she was. It wasn't thousands of years or anything, but she had lived years longer than any person she had read about. She was ugly and looked old from birth, there was nothing that was going to change that, but *inside*, oh inside she felt like she was twenty-eight. She never got sick; not even a sniffle. And there was a spring in her step that made her feel like the president of the Charles Kuralt fan club when he got to meet his other idol, the *other* guy in Culture Club. The one that wasn't Boy George.

The cookies not only had that effect on her, but on all of those who were lucky enough to be able to partake. Which were a very select few, admittedly; namely, a couple park rangers and a very peculiar talking squirrel. The park rangers would do anything to protect her, whether it meant directing the delivery trucks to her house, or keeping her house a secret from everyone else. Rick, in particular, was well past the age of retirement, but he felt as though he were a teenager. Retirement was completely out of the question. He didn't mind his job at all, plus he would have been denied access to the one thing that was keeping him feeling young and happy. The cookies were more perfect than any designer drug on the market, and any time he had gone without for longer than he should have, he felt his age quickly engulfing his body and mind. Incidentally, the talking squirrel still did what all talking squirrels did, but he did it with more enthusiasm than most. Also, he was thirty-eight years old.

"Oh, where are you?" she asked, as she checked the time. They were late. She was going to have to dock them their pay. Haha. That was a funny thought. Of course she had no intention of ever paying them. Or letting them leave.

The truck meandered its way through the forest, zigging this way and zagging that.

"How much farther, do you think?" asked Hansel to his navigating sister.

"About five more miles or so. We haven't gotten to the chocolate river yet."

Hansel applied the brakes.

"Why are you stopping?" Gretel asked.

He pointed out the driver's side window.

"Is that it?" she asked.

"I think so," he said, throwing his hazards on and stepping out of the vehicle.

Gretel jumped out of her side and raced to the river bank. "Holy cow, are you seeing this?"

Hansel nodded. It was indeed a river, about twelve feet or so across where they were standing, appearing to be made entirely of chocolate. It was dark and viscous and the smell drifting up was out of this world.

Gretel began disrobing.

"What are you doing?" Hansel asked.

"Going for a swim," she replied.

"We don't have time for that, sister. We have to get going or we're gonna be late."

"We're already late," she said. "When's the next chance we're gonna have to swim in a chocolate river?"

He thought about it. The way he felt about this trip and their chances of survival, the answer was probably never. But he stayed put as she dove in.

It took her a minute to surface, long enough for Hansel to become worried. But she did, her hair matted with liquid chocolate. "Woo-hoo," she shouted.

"How is it?" he asked.

"It feels wonderful. Like one of those expensive spa treatments or something. It's warm, and feels great on my skin. Come on, you should try it."

"No thanks," Hansel said.

"What's this?" she asked, and held out her hand. "Haha! Swedish fish. You've gotta be kidding me. It's like I'm on a Willie Wonka tour!"

"Yeah, well be careful. You know what happened to Gene Wilder."

"He turned into Johnny Depp and ruined a perfectly good movie?" she asked.

"Exactly. Friggin' Tim Burton. Now get on outta there. We gotta go."

"All right," she said, stepping out of the river. "Don't know why you're in such a hurry to race to our certain deaths anyway."

"Because this lady sounds like she's completely nuts. The less we piss her off, the better chance we have." Hansel handed her a towel. "Here. Dry off well. I don't need you tracking cacao all through the cab."

She toweled off and opened her door.

"Hold up," he said, and threw her a fresh towel. "Sit on this."

She put up one of her fingers. "Sit on this," she mumbled.

12. Delivery

Hansel drove until the road all but disappeared. "Are you sure this is right?" he asked Gretel.

"Positive. Says so right here on the map. Look, there's a sign."

She pointed out the window to a hand-written sign that said: DELIVERIES with an arrow pointing straight ahead.

"How does she expect anyone to get a truck through here?" said Hansel, as he pulled to a stop. "There's no road."

Gretel dialed the old woman, who picked up before it even rang.

"Hello?"

"Hi, this is Gretel. Your delivery driver?"

"Yes, yes," the old lady said impatiently. "Where are you?"

"We're by a delivery sign," said Gretel.

"Ah, you're here. Splendid!"

"Yes, but how do we get to your place? The road's gone."

"Keep driving straight. You'll see. It's only another quarter mile or so. Can't miss it. See you soon."

"What did she say?" asked Hansel.

"She said keep driving straight ahead."

"Fine, but if this truck gets all scratched up for driving down this nonexistent road, we're going to haggle with that old bitch. Nothing in the job description said anything about off-roading."

He kept on driving straight ahead, and as he did, the oddest thing was happening. The road was no longer disappearing. Nothing touched their truck. It was as though the trees and bramble that were seeming to block their way were just an illusion. The road was opening up to them mere feet in front of the truck. The road quickly ended in a very large field, with an odd-looking driveway winding its way around the side.

"Stop the truck," Gretel said.

"Now? Come on, I wanna get this over with."

"Just for a second. Something's weird."

She got out of the truck and bent down toward the driveway. Reaching down, she grabbed a handful of the gravel they were driving on, examined it closely, and took a bite.

"Stop eating dirt and get back in the truck," Hansel called.

She shook her head. "It's not dirt. It's crushed Oreos."

Hansel stepped out of the truck and grabbed himself a handful. He took a bite of his own and shook his head. "Not Oreos. Hydrox."

"Even better. And look how vibrant the grass is in the field. Wonder what it's made of." She pulled up a clump and stuffed it into her mouth.

"What is it?" he asked.

"It's grass," she said, spitting it out.

"Come on. Let's keep going."

They got back into the truck, drove around a little curve, and came upon the old lady's house. *House* was actually quite the understated word. They had originally expected a shack when they found out where the house was located, but this house was bigger than any that they had ever seen in person. Or on TV, for that matter. It had been well-camouflaged here in its spot in the woods, but how something this large could stay hidden from so many was an absolute wonder.

DELIVERIES IN BACK another sign said, and Hansel pulled the truck around to the rear of the building. He'd never seen a residence with its own loading dock before, but he was seeing one now.

"Let's switch," he said to Gretel. "You back it up."

"Oh, you're conceding the fact that I'm the better backer-upper?" she asked.

"If that's what you think," he said. "I just don't wanna hit anything on the building and end up owing this lady any more money than we do already."

"Fair enough. Still think you're conceding, though."

"Just back the damn thing up, wouldja?"

She backed the truck up and eased it to a gentle stop without ramming the building. "And that's how it's done," she said.

Hansel slow-clapped. "Here goes nothing," he said as he got out of the cab.

The door opened before he had a chance to ring the buzzer, and there stood before him a most hideous old lady. He couldn't help but think that she looked exactly like one of the witches in a children's fairytale. Diminutive in stature, scraggly gray hair that was just barely clinging to her scalp, sunken gray eyes, and a large, crooked nose complete with giant wart. To his surprise, she greeted him with a warm embrace, which was physically uncomfortable and bony, yet still felt nice, somehow. "Welcome!" she said cheerily.

"Hi. I'm Hansel. Sorry we're late."

"Oh, that's quite all right. The fact is, you made it." Gretel got out of the truck, and the old lady greeted her with a nice hug as well.

"Sorry we're late," she said.

"It's all right, love. I have all the time in the world, really. At least you got here. Now, let's see what kind of damage those horrible cookies did to your truck." She opened the door to the loading dock and examined the trailer door. She shook her head with a tsk-tsk. "My apologies," she said. "I suppose I should have warned you this could happen."

"You mean, this isn't the first time?" Gretel asked.

"Far from it. Luckily, it doesn't happen often, but it's certainly not a happy occasion when it does. Now, let's open it up and see what we have here."

Hansel undid the bed sheet that was keeping the door held shut and flung it open. Inside the trailer resembled the scene of a really demented horror movie. Cookie bits, shrink wrap, and busted pallets were scattered everywhere. And blood. So much blood.

The old lady gestured to the corner of the room. "Pallet jack's over there. Sorry I don't have a forklift. I always wanted one, but at this point in life, I fear it's too late to bother. Come on. Let's see what we can salvage."

As they were unloading the truck, Hansel spoke up. "Once again, I'm so, so sorry. Once we get this all unloaded and counted, we'll figure out who owes what to whom."

"It really is quite all right," she said. "It's not your fault. It's the damned company I get these cookies from. They promise freshness, but sometimes I think they're a little *too* fresh. They're never consistent. Sometimes they're perfect, and sometimes they ship them undercooked. It never used to be like this. The quality of American craftsmanship has really gone downhill. Next thing you know, I'll have to start buying them from Mexico or Venezuela. Way I see it, *they* owe *you* money for the damage to your truck. They really should have warned you about this."

Hansel had had enough beating around the bush. He decided to just come right out and ask it. "What's the deal with the cookies, anyway?"

"What ever do you mean, dear?" the old lady asked.

"Well, they don't seem, uh, normal. I mean, I'm not much of a sweets guy, but I have had the occasional cookie. And from what I remember, they don't normally twitch and bleed like these ones."

"It's the yeast," the old lady said.

"Yeast? In cookies?" Gretel asked. "I've never heard of yeast in cookies."

"I'm sorry," said the old lady. "I didn't realize you were a pastry chef."

"I'm not," said Gretel. "I just never heard of yeast in cookies."

"And that's why you've never seen cookies like these," said the lady. "Most use baking soda. This is why I order from this particular company. They're the only ones that use a similar recipe to my own. See, I used to do all my own baking. But it has just become too much for an old lady like myself to keep up with. Which reminds me, I need to preheat my oven."

She disappeared for a second, and when she came back, Hansel asked her a question.

"What's the deal with all the cookies, anyway? Why the obsession with them? I mean, you can't possibly eat them all."

"No no, dear," the old lady said. "I mean, I eat my fair share, believe me. But I don't eat all of them."

"So what do you do with them?" Gretel asked.

The old lady laughed. "My dear," she said, "just look around you."

She did, and so did Hansel. And for the first time they noticed that the entire house was not made of normal building materials.

"Your house is made of cookies?" Gretel asked.

The old lady nodded. She broke off a couple of pieces of one of the walls, and handed one piece each to Hansel and Gretel. "Go ahead," she said. "Take a bite."

Gretel took the first bite. "Forgive me for saying so," she said with a mouthful of very dry cookie, "it's a little stale."

"That's because it's very old," she said, as she watched Hansel take a bite of his own. "The real magic happens when you swallow it."

They both tried very hard to do just that, but it was impossible. Neither one of them could work up the saliva needed to force the cookies down.

"Come on," the old lady said, and put her arms around the siblings. "Let's leave this for now and go relax in the kitchen. I have some fresher cookies that just came out of the oven."

Hansel and Gretel looked at each other with a little trepidation.

"And milk," the old lady said.

"Now you're talking," said Gretel.

13. Magic

"Have a seat," the old lady said to the siblings. They each took a seat at the kitchen table.

The old lady pulled a jug of milk from the refrigerator. "What'll it be?" she asked. "Regular milk or chocolate?"

"Regular," said Hansel.

"Chocolate for me, please," said Gretel.

The old lady poured three glasses of milk, and stuck one of them under the faucet. She turned it on, and a thick, dark liquid poured out.

"Is that chocolate coming out of the tap?" Gretel asked.

"Sure is," the old lady said. "I have it piped in straight from the river."

"Amazing," said Gretel.

The old lady gathered some cookies on a paper plate and put them on the middle of the table. She took a seat next to Hansel. "Now," she said, "let's all enjoy this feast. Come on, dig in."

Gretel and Hansel each took a cookie from the plate. Cautiously, they looked at the old lady, who nodded. "Go on," said the lady. "They won't bite."

"You sure?" asked Hansel, and pointed to a mark on his leg. "Already got bit a couple times by these things."

"No no," said the old lady, "these are home made. They've long since passed the biting stage. I make sure all my cookies are properly dead, uh, cooked. You'll be fine." She took a bite of her own cookie just to prove she was telling the truth. "Mmmm," she said. "This is my best batch yet. Go on. You'll be glad you did."

Gretel looked at Hansel, and he took a bite. He nodded. "Actually," he said with his mouth full, "these are really good."

"See?" said the old lady. "Nothing to fear, dear. Go on, take a bite."

Gretel did as she was told. Hansel was right. It was delicious. They each took a sip of milk to wash it down. Seconds later, both Hansel and Gretel felt as though they had just taken several hits of ecstasy mixed with cocaine.

"Whoo!" said Hansel.

"Yowza!" said Gretel.

"Told you so. Don't you feel great?"

"Best I've felt in years," Hansel said, and scarfed the rest of the cookie down.

"Holy McMoley!" said Gretel, and shoved the rest of her cookie in her mouth, washing it down with a large gulp of chocolate milk.

"Okay, okay," said the old lady. "Slow down. These are quite potent." She shared her cookies to win their trust, and now that that had been accomplished, there was no reason for them to eat any more. It was a waste, considering what she had planned next. "Wait here," she said. "I'll be right back."

"You know," said Gretel, taking another bite of her cookie, "I have a pretty good feeling about this."

"Me too," said Hansel. "I think we'll be okay. I'm pretty sure all the rumors about truckers going missing were just that. Rumors."

"Yeah. She seems like a sweet lady," said Gretel.

"The sweetest," said Hansel.

"Hansel?" a voice called. "Gretel?"

Hansel looked at his sister. "Did you hear that?"

"You mean someone calling our names?"

"Yeah."

"Sure did."

"Sounded like it was coming from the warehouse," said Hansel.

"Probably the old lady," said Gretel.

"No," said Hansel. "It sounded like a man's voice."

"Well, let's face it," said Gretel, "she doesn't have the most feminine voice in the world. Too many cigarettes is my guess."

"Probably," said Hansel, "but this was even more masculine than her voice."

"Oh my," said Gretel. "What if the rumors *are* true? What if it's a missing truck driver?"

"One that happens to know our names?" asked Hansel.

"Well, you know," Gretel said, "I *am* a legendary backer-upper. Word's getting around."

"Whatever," said Hansel. "Let's go investigate."

"Hansel?" came the voice again. "Gretel?"

"Coming!" Gretel replied.

They entered the warehouse.

"Hansel?" called the voice. "Gretel?"

"We heard you the first time!" Hansel answered.

"Sounds like it's coming from over there." Gretel pointed to one of the pallets.

Hansel rushed to where the voice was coming from.

"Hello?" said Hansel.

"In here." The voice was coming from one of the boxes.

"Where are you?" asked Hansel.

"Right here," said the voice. Gretel identified which box, and pointed.

Hansel ripped the box open. He removed the layer of wax paper that was covering the cookies.

"Oh, I never thought I would see you again. My beautiful babies," said the voice. It was coming from one of the cookies. The thing looked normal enough, except peering out from the dead center was one familiar, rheumy-looking eye.

"Dad?" asked Gretel.

The eye grew wide. "Look out!" the cookie shouted, but it was too late. The back side of Gretel's head met with the business end of an old lady's rolling pin, and she collapsed to the floor.

"Gretel!" shouted Hansel.

"Gretel!" shouted the cookie. "Get her, son!"

Hansel wasted no time. He turned, facing the old lady, and pounced, knocking her to the floor. She reared back and cold-cocked him with her fist to the side of his face. For a frail old thing, she sure packed a wallop. He spit blood out onto the floor. He reached for the rolling pin, and she swung it out of the way. She swung again, aiming for his head, but missed. Hansel reached again, latching onto the rolling pin. With all his might, he yanked it out of the witch's hand, reared back, and whooped her upside of her head. Her eyes rolled up into her skull.

She may or may not have been dead, but it didn't matter. Hansel dragged her by her feet into the kitchen, kicked open the oven door, and shoved her inside. "No more missing truck drivers," said Hansel. "The buck stops here."

Hansel's question was answered. She wasn't dead. Her eyes flew open wide. "Fuck you," he said, which wasn't very original, but what else do you say in that situation? Her mouth opened and she let out a blood-curdling scream that shattered the air around him. Okay. *Now* she was dead.

He ran into the warehouse and to the side of his sister, who was stirring. Her eyes fluttered. "Hansel?" she asked.

"Shh, shh. I'm here. It's over now."

"Dad?" she asked.

"Gretel?' the cookie replied.

"Let's get out of here," Hansel said. He helped Gretel to her feet, making sure she was steady. He grabbed the box that contained his father, guided Gretel to the passenger seat of his truck, and got in. He started the engine and took off toward the front of the property.

He soon found out, however, that with the death of the old lady, so died the magic that surrounded her place. They were engulfed by thick woods. The road was gone. There was no way out.

Epilogue

The seconds turned into minutes, the minutes turned into hours, the hours turned into days, the days to weeks, the weeks to months, the months to years, the years to more years. Time went on and on and they were still there, Hansel, Gretel, and the cookie that they called "Dad". They subsisted entirely on a diet of cookies, both ordered in from the company they had originally delivered for, as well as ones baked from scratch, made using the old lady's secret recipe that was written out on an index card. Deliveries came in, truckers went missing, new additions were built onto the house; everything was the same as it was when the old witch lived here. So yes, the road did open back up eventually, but their desire to leave had vanished long before that. The cookies were amazing, and they had never felt better in their entire lives. One cookie they never ate, however, was their father. They fed him cookies of his own, which technically made him a cannibal, sure, but they also kept him alive and feeling magnificent. They only wished they could turn him back into the man they used to know, but that was beyond their capabilities. There was no turning back now. Their father would remain a cookie till the end of his days, and they would just have to get used to it.

"You know," said Cookiedad, laughing, "it's kind of funny."

"What's that, Pop?" Hansel asked.

"I sent you out into the world to make something of yourselves. To become adults and get you out of my hair. And now, here we are, together again."

"Nice, isn't it?" asked Gretel.

"*Nice?*" said Cookiedad. "Nice? I should have known from the start. You two are like boogers on a child's finger. I can't get rid of ya!"

And they all lived happily ever after.

THE END

OTHER BOOKS BY MARC RICHARD

THE NOVELS:
DEGREES OF SEPARATION
HARM'S WAY
THOSE EYES
IT'LL END IN TEARS

THE SERIES:
DAVE! (A Novel from the Future)
    PART 1: THE INVADERS
    PART 2: D.C.
    PART 3: ENDGAME

THE COLLECTIONS:
SIX OUT OF FIVE:
DAVE! THE FIRST TRILOGY
SORRY!
#sorrynotsorry (Fan Club Exclusive)

Go to www.marcrichardauthor.com for cool, free things

Printed in Great Britain
by Amazon